EXPOSING THE PAST

Also by Alice Zogg

Stand-Alone Mysteries

No Curtain Call
The Ill-Fated Scientist
Accidental Eyewitness
A Bet Turned Deadly

R. A. Huber Mysteries

Evil at Shore Haven
Guilty or Not
Murder at the Cubbyhole
Revamp Camp
Final Stop Albuquerque
The Fall of Optimum House
The Lonesome Autocrat
Tracking Backward
Turn the Joker Around
Reaching Checkmate

EXPOSING THE PAST

ALICE ZOGG

aventine press

This book is a work of fiction.

Published by Aventine Press
55 East Emerson St.
Chula Vista CA 91911
www.aventinepress.com

ISBN: 978-1-59330-978-7

Library of Congress Control Number: 2020911968
Library of Congress Cataloging-in-Publication Data
EXPOSING THE PAST/Alice Zogg
Printed in the United States of America

To my niece, Gabi

CREDITS

Gayle Bartos-Pool wore two hats when assisting me with this story. She gave me tips on how to obtain ancestry DNA testing and, again, did a great job of editing my manuscript. I appreciate your dedication, Gayle. As with my previous books, I counted on my daughter Franziska for proofreading and thank her for taking the time, despite her busy schedule. My gratitude goes out to the members of the Los Angeles chapter of Sisters in Crime. Their support keeps me focused on the craft of writing. Here is where in previous books I gave tribute to my husband, Wilfried, for his help with scouting out locations. There was no need for that with this one; San Remo does not exist. I took the liberty of placing the fictional town smack between La Cañada Flintridge and Pasadena.

CHAPTER 1

Had Sherry Rinaldi not run into her Doppelgänger on that fateful day on Maui, Hawaii, she could have avoided all the misery that digging up the past brought.

She and her husband, Dave, were celebrating their 15th wedding anniversary on the island. Since Sherry was a foreign language high school teacher, the two had picked their wedding date and honeymoon at the end of the schoolyear in June. They did so now with their anniversary getaway one-and-a-half decades later. The ten days of bliss - - snorkeling, swimming, boating, and playing golf - - ended with a luau in the hotel gardens.

The traditional "pig in the ground" had roasted for many hours, turning out mouthwatering in the end. And equally delicious was the huli-huli chicken, poi, mango bread, and sticky rice. Sherry had finished her dessert of Hawaiian pudding kulolo and went inside the hotel to use the restroom. Rather than taking the time to go all the way to their own room, she opted to use the hotel's facility next to the lobby.

In the ladies room, she glanced up to the mirror while washing her hands and froze. Dare she trust her eyes? Two images of herself stared back at her. At that instant, the woman freshening up at the sink next to her made the same eerie discovery.

They turned to face each other, stunned by their striking likeness. They both had light-blue eyes and exaggerated arched brows, an oval-shaped face, and a turned-up nose. Their bone structure was identical. They even wore their blondish hair the same way, tied up in a bun at the crown of the head.

The one difference was their outfits. Sherry wore a turquoise wrap-around skirt with a white blouse and the stranger was clad in a flowery Hawaiian dress.

The other woman recovered first, laughed with a deep chuckle, and burst out, "If I didn't know any better, I'd say we were related!"

"Yeah, like twins," Sherry agreed, trying not to seem freaked out.

The other woman extended a hand, "I'm Kirsten."

Sherry shook it and likewise introduced herself.

"Where are you from?" her double asked.

"Pasadena in Southern California. And you?"

"What a coincidence! I spent my first few years near there. Now I live in San Diego. We're flying home tomorrow."

"It's my last night here too."

They seemed tongue-tied at that point, dried their hands, refreshed their lipsticks, said "bon voyage," and walked out of the ladies room together.

The young man at the concierge desk in the lobby called out, "A moment please, Mrs. Hiller! We have a message for you." Kirsten stopped by his desk as the other walked on.

By the time Sherry rejoined Dave in the garden, the luau had progressed to the entertainment part. Instead of enjoying the performance of the hula dancers, she could not get the image of Kirsten out of her mind and was passive and absent-minded for the rest of the evening.

****

After turning in on that final night in Hawaii and ready to switch off the light, Dave said, "What's wrong?"

"What makes you think something is?"

"Come now. You haven't been yourself since going to the bathroom during the luau. Are you sick or did something happen?"

Reluctantly, she told him about her experience.

He laughed and said, "Is that all? You met your double and no longer can consider yourself unique!"

"Don't make fun! It's extremely disturbing. She looked exactly like me. She even wore her hair in the same type of a bun. I can't begin to describe what a shock it was."

Always ready to joke, he winked at his wife, with her long hair combed and hanging loose, and remarked, "Your clone probably also takes her shock of hair down before going to bed."

CHAPTER 2

On the plane ride home, the couple was preoccupied with individual musing. Dave had a master's degree in engineering and worked at a major electronics company. His thoughts were already plagued with the work piling up at his desk. Would he be able to catch up or was he going to have to work overtime to meet deadlines?

Sherry had had trouble sleeping the night before, mulling over her restroom encounter. She now tried to get some shuteye, but it was no use. The image of Kirsten crept into her mind's eye, laughing and declaring, "If I didn't know any better, I'd say we were related!"

She now considered, what if I have a sister and a twin at that? Dad had always been vague about her early years, and her older brother had not been of much help on the few occasions when she had inquired into their past. She was two when her mom died, and all she had was a picture to remember her by. Could there have been a third child that Dad had given away, unable to cope with bringing up such a large family on his own?

Why should she bother at this point? She was 42 years old, had been raised by a loving father, was married to a great guy, had no children to worry about except for the ones in her classroom, and was in perfect shape and health. So why dwell on the past? She could not answer the question, but the Kirsten thing wouldn't leave her any peace of mind. There was one trait of herself she knew to be a fact: Unfinished business drove her crazy.

Dave suddenly asked, "Are you going to tutor again this summer?"

"I have one person, an adult, lined up for Monday. He got a job offer in Munich, Germany, and wants a quick introduction to the German language. I'll teach him the basics, and he plans to study vocabulary on his own. The man is pressed for time, so a few lessons next week should do it. As for the rest, I may skip tutoring altogether this year."

Sherry had no idea why she made that statement, but now that it was out, a plan started to form in her mind about how she would spend the rest of the summer.

Dave knew his wife well enough to guess what went on in that gorgeous, smart head of hers. He cringed inwardly, grasping that the months ahead would not be easy if his assumption was correct.

He gave her an encouraging smile and said, "I read someplace that we all have a double, whether or not we ever meet that person. The lookalike is random and has nothing to do with being related. It's a fluke of nature."

"You're just saying that to make me feel better," Sherry shot back. "It wasn't only a likeness; we looked identical."

"What are you suggesting?"

Sherry looked him in the eye and stated, "I don't have a choice but need to get to the bottom of it." That said, she turned her face away and stared out the window, seeing nothing but clouds.

By the time they landed at LAX, she had made a mental outline of her plan of action.

CHAPTER 3

On Monday, June 22, the adult student promptly arrived at 7:00 p.m. at the Rinaldi residence, a single-level Spanish style home in a middle-class neighborhood of Pasadena. Sherry was clearing away the last dinner dish when the doorbell rang.

They got comfortable in the den, where she opened a notebook sitting at the ready on the coffee table.

Her student glanced at the stationary bicycle erected at one corner of the room and remarked, "I'm thinking of getting one of those." Then he got down to business and said, "I bought a textbook and taught myself some vocabulary already. I'm mostly interested in learning some simple conversational German. My work colleagues in Munich speak English, but I think it would be great if I could understand and converse a bit in their language."

"I agree. You would make a good impression, showing incentive to assimilate," said Sherry.

Then she scribbled three little words onto the first page of the notebook - - *der, die, das* - - and stated, "Let's start with some basic grammar. Different from the English language, where the only definite article is the word 'the,' in German there are three; *der, die, das*. This is because the nouns have a gender and take the articles, *der* (masculine), *die* (feminine), and *das* (neuter.) For example: *Der Hund, die Katze, das Mädchen*. Even if the cat is male, it is still '*die* Katze.' 'Mädchen' is a girl but takes nonetheless the article '*das*' because the noun is neuter. By the same token, 'Doppelgänger' is a masculine noun and takes the article '*der*', regardless if it happens to be a woman."

Sherry got a hold of herself, thinking, listen to me! I can't even teach beginner German without lapsing into my obsession.

Confused, the man stared at her, having been lost at the half-way mark of the example.

For the next 90 minutes, Sherry concentrated on teaching. She covered indefinite articles, verb conjugation and tenses, the difference between strong and weak verbs, and basic parts of speech. She admitted that because of its gendered nouns, German grammar was a bit tricky and stressed that he should memorize the gender of each new word learned, immediately.

Then she looked at her watch and said, "That's it for now. In your next lesson we'll cover conversation and pronunciation. German words are relatively easy to pronounce. You might have a little difficulty with the ü's, ä's, and ö's, but the rest is a piece of cake."

At the door he turned to her and asked, "You teach other languages as well?"

"Sure. French and Spanish. Why?"

"I know someone who wants to learn French."

"I'm taking the summer off. If the person can wait until Christmas or spring break, I'm available."

CHAPTER 4

Sherry jumped into action the next day by first tackling her brother, Ben. She texted him with the request that he'd call her when he had time for a long discussion.

He called in the evening and said, "What's up, Sis?"

"Try to remember stuff from when we were kids. I mean, way back before Mom died."

"You're kidding! What brings this on?"

"Never mind. Think back, was there another girl in our family?"

"Of course not. There was only you and me. Are you hallucinating?"

"I'm being serious. I was two when Mom died and can't remember that far back, but you were close to five. *You* should be able to remember. So please think hard, Ben, was there another kid either before, at the same time, or after I came along?"

There was a long pause on the line. Then Ben said, "Are you suggesting that Mom had another baby besides you and it died?"

"No, that's not it. And never mind why I'm asking; I have good reason. Close your eyes and think back to the days before Mom drowned and the time immediately afterward. Was there another little girl with us?"

"Before Mom's accident, there were the four of us. Later, I remember that we had a nanny while Dad went to work, but there was no other kid. Wait! Our cousin - - can't remember her name - - was around a lot. I guess to keep you company."

"How old was she?"

"Don't know. Maybe your age, maybe older."

Sherry said, "As far as I know, we only have one girl cousin and that's Terri."

"It wasn't Terri. Maybe she was a neighbor's kid that hung around and I thought it was a cousin. We lived in a big apartment complex at the time, remember?"

"No, I don't remember. That's why I'm asking you."

"When Mom was alive, and for a short time afterwards, we lived in an apartment before Dad bought the house in San Remo."

"Where was the apartment complex?"

"Also in San Remo, I believe. Ask Dad."

"Oh, I will." And she said, "I do remember the nanny, though. She talked funny. Was her name Margit?"

"Yeah, that's right, and she had an accent. She lived with us in the house and then one day, all of a sudden, she was gone."

Sherry said, "Something else that always puzzled me. Mom could swim, right?"

"She loved to swim and took us to the apartment pool a lot. She taught me how and was starting to teach you."

"So why did she drown if she was a good swimmer? Dad was always elusive when I asked for details about her drowning accident."

"I'm not sure but think she bumped her head and knocked herself unconscious. It happened at night when she was alone in the pool."

Preventing her brother from asking again what this was about, Sherry quickly inquired how her niece and nephew were doing. She learned that Ben's daughter had scored high on her PSAT test and that they would be scouting out colleges soon. Another bit of news was his son playing a trumpet solo at his middle school end-of-year concert.

"Sorry we had to miss the concert," she said.

"You didn't give me a chance to ask. How was Hawaii?"

"Wonderful!" said Sherry. And without missing a beat she asked, "Was she blond?"

"What?"

"The girl that hung around with us."

"How should I remember the color of her hair? That was some 40 years ago when I was between three and five!"

"You're right, that was a dumb question. Forget it."

Then she asked, "How many pictures do you have of our mom?"

"Not many. Why?"

"I have a single one where she's sitting on a sofa with you on her side and me in her arms when I was an infant. It's a black-and-white photo."

"Yeah, I've seen that one."

"Do you have any pictures of her in color?"

"Could be, but I can't say for sure. I'd have to dig up some real old ones."

"Please do when you get a chance."

"Are you going to tell me what's going on?" he asked.

"Maybe some other day, but please do me a favor and look for more pictures of her," she replied and ended the call.

CHAPTER 5

Max Andino, Sherry's father, had recently retired from his job as CFO at an advertising company. At 70, he was not ready for the rocking chair yet, went for daily brisk walks around his Arcadia neighborhood, and played a round of golf on occasion. He never remarried after the tragic loss of his wife but had had a string of women friends in the course of the last 40 years. Following breakfast on Wednesday morning, June 24, he was absorbed in the *L. A. Times*, preferring to hold a paper rather than getting the news online.

Vanessa, his current girlfriend, silently entered the kitchen, cleared away the empty plate he had shoved to the side, and said, "I'm off to work."

Max lowered the paper so that not only his unruly mop of white hair but the rest of his classic profile became visible. He peered at her over the reading glasses perched on the tip of his nose and said, "It's that late already?"

"Yep, got to run." She stepped closer and gave him a peck on the forehead, stating, "You need a haircut." And then, "We'll meet for lunch?"

"Sorry. Sherry has claimed me already."

"Oh?"

"She wants to have a private talk. Can't imagine what about."

"Probably to complain that I'm taking up too much of your time," she said, and walked toward the door.

He watched her leave the room with a wiggle of her *derrière* and thought, the woman's still got it! At, what, maybe 60? That was an educated guess. She had never revealed her age to him and could be anything from 55 upward.

****

The lunch rendezvous took place in Old Town Pasadena. Sherry got to the restaurant first, was shown to a table, and then sat there rehearsing the subject she was going to bring up with her dad. Since he had never liked talking about the past, she assumed that it was too painful for him. In her teens, she had tried to get a picture of what her mom had been like, but when questioned, he had always managed to steer the talk in a different direction.

Max spotted his daughter and walked to their table with big strides, bent down for a bear hug, and then seated himself across from her. He said, "Hi, Poker! I take it you had a good time in Hawaii. You even have a hint of a tan."

"I must have inherited some of your genes after all," she remarked. And studying him, added, "You look good yourself. Retirement agrees with you."

"I'm bored already and mulling over getting myself a paid hobby."

"As long as it doesn't involve the Greek mafia," she teased.

"I'm thinking more along the lines of a financial advisor."

They gave their orders of Reuben sandwiches, a glass of Riesling for him, and water for her.

As soon as the waitress was out of earshot Max said, "Okay, Poker, let's cut the small talk. There's a reason you summoned me. What are you poking around in?"

She shrieked, "Don't call me that. I'm not your little Poker any longer; I'm a grown woman." As soon as they were out, she regretted her harsh words but it was too late to take them back.

He tried to hide his hurt feelings by saying, "I've always meant 'Poker' as an endearment, but I'll skip it from now on. So Sherry, what's up?"

"First off, we lived in an apartment complex when Mom was alive, right?"

"Correct."

"What was the name of the place and where is it, if it still exists?"

"The Acorn Forest Apartments in San Remo and, as far as I know, they're still there."

Sherry braced herself before saying, "I know that you hate talking about it, but you never told me the details about Mom's drowning accident."

"What's all this about?" he questioned. "Are you planning to write your memoir like everyone is doing these days?"

"Maybe, but I'd like to know for my own satisfaction."

With sudden sadness he gave in and said, "I thought we covered this a long time ago, but here is what happened. Your mother swam laps in the complex's pool most nights before going to bed. She never wanted me to join her. This was not because someone needed to stay put to take care of you and your brother - - you kids hardly needed supervision tucked in bed asleep - - but she cherished the time to herself.

"On that particular night we had an argument before she stormed off toward the pool area in her bathing suit. I later blamed myself for not going after her. At the time, though, I was mad and went to bed. I woke up around 2:00 a.m. the next morning and, realizing she was not in bed next to me, I got dressed and went out looking for her."

His words softened nearly to a whisper as he continued, "I spotted her at the bottom of the pool and jumped in, clothed and in shoes, but it was too late. She'd been dead for hours."

Sherry gripped both his hands and said, "I'm so sorry, Dad."

He shook them free and said, "Let me finish, since you want to know the details. There was an extensive head wound. The medical examiner determined that she had crashed head-on into the edge at the end of the pool during a turnaround of her lap swimming, rendering her unconscious. My take on this has always been that she was so angry that she swam herself into a frenzy. At that late hour your mother had been the sole person out for a swim, so no one witnessed her drowning and could come to the rescue."

Her eyes moist with compassion, she said, "Thanks for sharing, I know this was extremely hard for you." And after a long silence she continued, "We must have moved to our house soon afterwards, since I have no recollection of the apartments at all."

"You were too young to remember living there. Your mother and I had looked into the housing market around that time, figuring out the financing and all. After what happened, I couldn't stomach staying in the place and looked for a house in the area. I was lucky to find a suitable one right away, and we moved in as soon as it closed escrow. In the short time we remained at Acorn Forest, I avoided the pool area like the plague."

"How long did we have Margit, the nanny?"

He smiled and said, "So you do remember Margit. She was a Godsend and stayed with us for about two years until you started preschool and I put you and Ben in afterschool daycare."

Sherry remarked, "Ben said she left us suddenly."

"Oh, did he? It must have felt that way to a child. In actuality, I no longer needed her and let her go."

"Have you kept in touch with her?"

"No. She went back to Norway, where she was from."

Their sandwiches had long been served but neither had much of an appetite. They forced themselves now to eat a few bites while brooding over the talk they'd had. Max re-lived the horror again, something he had tried to avoid for decades. Sherry struggled with mixed feelings. On the one hand she was glad that Dad had finally talked straight about what had happened. On the other, she felt sorry for him.

Still, needing to know the truth, she said, "You've been a loving father and did a great job of bringing Ben and me up all on your own. I'm grateful for that. But tell me, was there another sibling whom you couldn't cope with raising, and instead gave her up for adoption?"

"What the devil gave you that idea?"

"Never mind, but is it true? Do I have a sister or even a twin?"

"Certainly not! Your suggestion is absurd. Your mother and I had Ben and you, period. There was no other kid." He stared at her with a look that demanded an explanation.

She said, "I met a woman who looks exactly like me."

"So that's what this is all about."

After a moment's hesitation he said, "Doubles are common and it doesn't mean the lookalikes are related. So please Po - - I mean Sherry, don't lose any sleep over it."

Nothing more was said about the subject. They finished their lunch, which Max insisted on paying, and then went their separate ways.

CHAPTER 6

Sherry didn't think her dad would lie to her. However, deep down in her gut she knew there was a mystery tying the Kirsten woman to her. She also knew that there would be no peace for her until she got to the bottom of it. For starters, she needed to scout out the territory.

San Remo was a small town nestled at the foot of the San Gabriel Mountains, close to La Cañada Flintridge on its western border and Pasadena on its east. The Acorn Forest Apartments were located on one of the main streets at the center of town. She had been driven by them umpteen times when growing up, on her way to school or running errands with her dad but had had no idea or recollection of once having lived there.

She parked her car on the street and then walked into the complex. There were no acorns, let alone a forest. Trees and flowerbeds were spread out between buildings, but the place looked typically urban. Close to the entrance stood rows of mailboxes and to their right was a sandy playground with equipment set off a small structure that housed the laundry room. How convenient, Sherry thought. People could watch their toddlers on the swings while tending to their laundry.

At a distance to the left was a large, gated pool with a shallow wading pool for small kids next to it. The resident parking spaces were in the center of the complex, surrounded by five two-story apartment buildings, identified with big letters on their facade as A through E. Sherry noticed a sign above the mail boxes that read, *Manager's office in building A at ground level*, and headed that way.

Calling the space an office was a stretch. It was nothing more than a cranny, housing a desk with a desktop computer and monitor. An open door gave access to the manager's own living quarters. She heard banging coming from somewhere beyond that door. When the noise stopped for a second, she cleared her throat.

Someone with a baritone yelled, "Be right with you!" And the hammering continued.

A couple of minutes later, she met the person belonging to the voice. He was a robust man in his late fifties, wearing cargo pants and a t-shirt. He gave the impression of being able to fix anything, from malfunctioning garbage disposals to leaking roofs, and anything in-between.

He said, "Sorry, I couldn't drop what I was doing, but now I'm all yours. Are you looking to rent an apartment? There's a two-bedroom available right now."

"Not really," Sherry said, "I'm wondering if you can help me. Are you by chance keeping a list of former tenants? You see, I used to live here and would like to get in touch with people who lived in these apartments at the same time."

"How long ago are you talking about?"

"Forty to forty-two years."

He burst into a deep, throaty laugh and said, "You must be kidding! That was at least five or six managers before me. We don't keep records from that far back. Besides, you're talking about a time before computers. You can't honestly believe that anyone would keep paperwork that long." He added, "And even if the records still existed, I wouldn't be allowed to give out the information."

Studying her, he said, "I'm surprised you were already around some forty years ago. And why is this important to you?"

Sherry looked out the small window with a view to the pool and, pointing to it, said, "I was two when my mom drowned over there and hoped to talk to some people who knew her."

Shocked, the manager said, "I was unaware that there had ever been a drowning in our pool. I'm so sorry."

"Naturally I don't remember her, but it would be nice to talk to some friends she may have made here."

He was sincere when he said, "I'm sorry that I can't help you."

"There's got to be a way to find some of those old tenants, but thanks anyway for listening to me."

She was already out the office door when he called after her, "Maybe you could put an ad in the paper. But don't mention the drowning, that would ruin Acorn Forest's reputation."

CHAPTER 7

Dave Rinaldi had experienced a particularly tiresome day on Friday, June 26. He was burdened with a heavy workload, trying to meet deadlines. And adding to his stress was the company politics employees were trying to get him involved in, regardless that he had no time or desire to participate. Dismissing his co-workers' meddling with a joke no longer did the trick. They wanted him to take sides, a thing he tried to avoid at all cost. On that Friday, he stayed and worked an extra hour in peace after everyone had left. His 16-mile commute from Studio City to his home in Pasadena, which on average took about 20 minutes, took twice as long that night because of an accident on the 134 freeway.

When he got home, Sherry was in the den giving her adult student his third and last German lesson. Dave found a note on the kitchen counter which read, *I made chicken stir-fry with veggies. It's in the fridge.* He heated it up in the microwave and ate alone.

Dave was half asleep when Sherry joined him in the living room watching the ten o'clock news but perked right up when seeing her. He hoped to get friendly with his wife as they went to bed, knowing that it would relax him after his stressful day. But it was not meant to be. Sherry was rigid as a telephone pole in his arms.

"What's making you upset?" he asked.

"Frustrated is more like it," she replied, and told him about her task which had led nowhere, so far.

She elaborated, "Ben was of no use and can't remember much, even though he was already five. From Dad I finally got a straight answer about Mom's drowning. As gratifying as that may be for me, it doesn't help with what I'm trying to ferret out. Yesterday, I was full of expectation when driving to the Acorn Forest Apartments in San Remo. The manager there was nice, and I hoped that he could direct me to some people who lived there at the time. That was too much to expect so many years later."

Dave was tempted to tell her to let it go. Even if a sibling of hers should exist - - and he didn't believe so for a moment - - what would be the point? They were both adults now with lives of their own. But he knew his wife well enough to understand that she was on a quest and could not let it rest until she knew the truth, one way or another.

She continued, "Where do I go from here? Facebook and Twitter are out of the question to get in touch with former apartment tenants. I would need names to go that route. Call it woman's intuition, but I'm positive that somebody - - or even more than one person - - who lived there at the crucial time knows something. I don't want to pressure Dad further. Besides, I'm sure he doesn't keep in touch with anyone from that time. He made it clear that he wanted to forget Acorn Forest and all its people."

She punched her pillow in irritation and said, "Darn it, there's got to be a way to get a hold of them. The manager suggested I should put an ad in the paper, but who reads the newspaper anymore?"

Dave said, "Hold on! That's not such a bad idea. Most of these people would be in their sixties, seventies, or even eighties by now. They are of the paper-reading generation."

"You're right. Dad gets the *L. A. Times* delivered daily; he wouldn't dream of reading the news online. It's worth a try. You're a genius."

She smacked a kiss on his cheek, turned her back to him, and stated, "I can sleep now. Good night, Hon."

Getting friendly was not meant to be that particular night.

CHAPTER 8

Sherry did two things the next day, Saturday. She placed an ad in the *Los Angeles Times* and was assured that it would run in the Sunday edition. She also placed it in a local Pasadena paper for good measure.

The piece was listed under the heading, *Town of San Remo* and it read, *"Attention former Acorn Forest Apartments tenants. If you lived in the above-mentioned apartment complex in the town of San Remo in the late 1970's to early 1980's, I would appreciate a chat with you."*

She left her e-mail address as contact information.

The second thing she did was research Kirsten, since she wanted to get in touch with her. What had the man at the concierge desk of the hotel in Hawaii called her? She saw him clearly mention to Kirsten, "Mrs. So-and-so, we have a message for you." Now, what was the name he called her by? Some easy name, like Muller, Ridder, or Miller. She couldn't remember. It will come to me, she told herself, and tried not to stress over it.

She was vigorously peddling on her stationary bicycle two hours later when it came to her, all of a sudden. Mrs.

Hiller! That's it. She jumped off the bike and went online to do the search. Thanks to the internet it was easy and fast nowadays to find someone when equipped with a first and last name. There were several people living in San Diego with the last name of Hiller but only one Kirsten Hiller. The birthdate, making her current age 43, was also a fit. BINGO, Sherry said aloud.

Her first impulse was to try to friend her on Facebook but she changed her mind. Making contact via social media would jeopardize Kirsten's privacy as well as her own. The phone was not a practical choice, given the fear of telemarketers and scammers. Unfortunately, she did not have her e-mail address.

That left the option of composing and mailing an old-fashioned letter. She decided that a handwritten correspondence would make a more personal impression than a typewritten one. So she went in search of stationery paper.

Sherry could not remember the last time she'd written such a letter but put herself to the task immediately. She had always been good with words, whether in her native English or a foreign language, but now had difficulty reaching the right tone. She didn't want to come across as either pushy or out of line, and most of all, didn't want to sound needy. It was also important that her note did not imply that she was jumping to conclusions. She wrote numerous drafts, with most of them landing in the wastebasket.

She started the heading over more than once, trying forms of address like, *"Hello, Doppelgänger; Hi there, Lookalike;* and *Dear Double.* She ended up simply using the woman's name. The last draft of the letter and the one she mailed read,

"*Dear Kirsten,*

"*Every so often, I think about meeting you in that hotel restroom. Does this happen to you also, I wonder? Our resemblance is striking, but is it possible that we have more in common than looks? I remember your words, 'If I didn't know any better, I'd say we were related!' Could we be?*

"*I would be interested to know more about you. You mentioned that you grew up near Pasadena. In what town, exactly? I know that you are married. Do you have children, what is your profession, and what hobbies are you pursuing?*

"*Here are some of my basics; I'm 42 years old, married, with no children. I'm a foreign language teacher at a high school here in Pasadena. My hobbies are sewing, skiing, and hiking. As to lineage, I have Greek ancestors on my father's side and am not sure about my mother's background.*

"*I would love to hear from you.*

"*Best wishes,*

"*Sherry Andino-Rinaldi*"

Signing with her maiden name was an afterthought. She added her two phone numbers, e-mail address, and street address.

****

Dave found his wife in a contented mood in the late afternoon that Saturday after returning from a round of golf with his buddies.

He said, "You seem at peace with yourself again!"

Sherry nodded. "I've taken your advice to place that ad in the paper and also wrote a letter to my Doppelgänger. It took me forever to compose that letter, and I had second thoughts while writing it, but now I feel satisfied. If I get a response to either or both, I'll go from there. If not, I'll drop the whole thing and be done with it."

"Good plan!" Dave agreed and thought, in particular the one about dropping it.

CHAPTER 9

Sunday evening, Bob Tully and his longtime partner, Ralph, returned to their home in South Pasadena from a long day of orchestrating a wedding at the country club. It had been meant to be an outdoor ceremony and reception but due to a sudden drizzle, had to be moved indoors at the last minute.

Bob and Ralph had been together for decades, both as domestic and business partners. They owned an event-planning-and-organizing outfit and had earned a reputation of excellence in that field. Bob, as an interior decorator, had brought his creativity and eye for detail to the table, whereas Ralph, a business major, was a born entrepreneur. They planned anything from birthday parties, weddings, anniversaries, bar mitzvahs/bat mitzvahs, and special occasion parties to family or class reunions. There was balance in their personal relationship, Bob being a dreamer and Ralph a realist.

Ralph said, "I'm beat. We sure had to hustle today, changing the venue at a moment's notice."

Bob, always the optimist, remarked, "True, but the wedding was a success nonetheless."

"Whether or not the young couple's marriage will be a success is another matter."

"That's out of our control, but I wish them the best."

"A good thing there was enough food leftover from the reception for us. I wouldn't be up to cooking dinner tonight." And getting back to complaining about the weather he said, "June gloom better be over by next Saturday. We have a July 4th beach party on the agenda."

Bob stated, "For sure it's over. It never rains on Independence Day."

Each had his own way of unwinding after a big job. As usual, Ralph sat in his recliner in the study and watched one of his favorite shows on Netflix, while Bob preferred reading a novel. On this particular night, though, he sat in the dining room and opened up the *L. A. Times*, having had no time in the morning to do so. He always browsed the obituaries before getting to the headlines and news, on the slight chance that he knew one of the departed.

Something caught his eye and he hollered, "Hey, Ralph, come here for a sec!"

The latter pressed "pause" on the remote and walked over to the dining room where his partner sat, staring at the open paper.

"Someone we know died?" he asked.

"No. Don't look at the obituaries." Bob put a finger by the ad on the adjacent page, saying, "What do you make of this?"

Ralph read the short announcement and commented, "So? Somebody is looking for tenants who lived in some apartments in San Remo a long time ago. What's so interesting about that?"

"I'm one of the tenants."

"Really? You never told me you'd lived in San Remo."

"It was a long time ago, way before we knew each other. I lived there from June of 1977 until September 1980, at which time I moved in with my first love."

"You never told me about that either!"

"Must have skipped my mind," Bob said with a chuckle. "So tell me already, what do you make of the ad?"

"Sounds fishy to me. I have no idea what it means, but don't answer it. The person didn't even have the decency to put a name on the piece."

"The name seems to be in the e-mail address but I don't know any Rinaldis. I'm curious, though."

"My advice is to ignore it and forget it. For all you know, the person may want to scam people and take their money."

Bob said, "It can't hurt to send an e-mail to find out what it's all about. Maybe I'm due an inheritance and the last record these people have of me was when I lived in those apartments."

"You're nuts!"

"Okay, that's improbable, but what if this Rinaldi person is a former tenant and wants to plan a reunion with fellow apartment residents of 40 years ago? You've got to admit that's possible, and it might even give us some business!"

"Do what you want but be careful."

That said, Ralph headed back to the study, while Bob had second thoughts. Did he need to take Ralph's warning seriously about the ad being a scam? I'll sleep on it, he told himself.

CHAPTER 10

At 43, Kirsten Hiller was in a good marriage, had two kids - - a boy of 13 and a girl of 11 - - and enjoyed her job as a real estate agent. In short, she had a busy but gratifying life. On Tuesday, June 30, she sat in her car on a side street near her son's year-round middle school in San Diego, waiting for him to get out. She couldn't help it, but her mind crept back to the letter she'd received. Already earlier, when chauffeuring her daughter and friends to dance lessons, the girls' chatter didn't prevent her from thinking about it.

There was a constant stream of kids walking by, but her son was not among them. What's keeping Alex, she thought, checking her watch. She was ready to send her son a text when she saw him coming at a run in her rearview mirror.

He tossed his backpack onto the car floor of the passenger seat and was about to get in when Kirsten stopped him and said, "Your coach informed me that soccer practice is 30 minutes earlier today. You had better get in the back seat and change. There's no time to drive home first. Your stuff is in the paper bag."

Alex changed into his practice uniform and cleats, saying, "Sorry, Mom, I had to make a quick stop at the school library."

"No problem. The coach can't expect everyone to get there on time on such short notice."

As she started the engine, her mind was already back to the letter from the woman she'd met in Hawaii. Did that person honestly think that they might be related? If so, it would be a distant relationship. Nobody in her family had ever mentioned a Sherry Andino-Rinaldi. And even if by chance there was a link way back in their ancestry, why care? She could not figure out the woman's motivation for contacting her. We look alike; so what?

She gave herself a mental slap on the head and thought, stop it already! Determined not to dwell on the woman's letter any longer, she asked her son, "So how was your day?"

"Okay, I guess," he replied. For a second she'd forgotten that one could not hold a conversation longer than a heartbeat with a teen.

When she dropped him off at the soccer field, it was time to drive back the way she'd come to pick up her daughter, Ella, from the dance studio.

****

At night, all was quiet at the Hillers' house when Mike came home from his 48-hour shift as a firefighter. The kids were in bed and Kirsten sat at the computer in the part of the den she called her office.

"What are you doing?" he asked, bending down to kiss her neck.

"Going over the latest listings, but it can wait." She swiveled around to face him and stated, "You look beat. I saw the structure fire on the news; were you there?"

"Yep, it was a challenge, but we got it under control."

"Hungry?"

"Nope. I showered and ate at the station but need to unwind a bit in front of the TV before going upstairs."

She held him back and said, "Don't go yet, I need your advice."

"What's up?"

"Remember when I told you about bumping into a woman that looked like me in the hotel restroom in Hawaii?"

"Vaguely. Why?"

She handed him the letter that was sitting open-faced on her desk, and said, "This came in today's mail. I don't know how she found our address. I'm positive I never mentioned my last name."

Mike read it. Then he went over it a second time and remarked, "Sounds like the woman is either bored or desperate to make you her friend."

"That's what you get out of her letter?"

"Yeah. Looks to me like having no kids and being a teacher, she has nothing much to do all summer than chase after a double she came across in Hawaii."

Kirsten said, "I think it goes deeper than that. After we stared at each other in the bathroom mirror in Hawaii,

I joked about being related, but she obviously took it to heart. She's suggesting that we may be carrying the same genes and wants to explore the possibility. In my opinion, that is why she's asking all those personal questions and gave me a bit of information about her own background."

"Okay, let's say you're right about her motivation. What difference does it make to you? Even if the woman is correct, it would be of no importance. You've lived 40-some years perfectly fine without knowing you may have a distant relation never seen or heard of before. And if it would be proven as fact, I doubt that the two of you would start a close friendship. Pasadena is not exactly around the corner from San Diego."

"True, but I'm curious now."

Mike asked, "Did you ever give the woman another thought before you received this letter?"

"Frankly, I'm too busy and it slipped my mind."

"There's your answer. Shred the letter and forget about it," Mike said, and walked out of her office.

Kirsten would try to forget about it but could not bring herself to feed it into the shredder. She tucked it away in her desk drawer instead and followed him to the living room.

CHAPTER 11

Sherry's life went on. The 4th of July weekend, with the highlight of watching the Rose Bowl Fireworks, had come and gone. She now concentrated on tasks she was too busy to accomplish during the school year, like cleaning out and re-lining the kitchen cupboards, and going through clothing closets to sort out garments for the Goodwill.

Ten days had passed since she had placed the ads and mailed the letter to Kirsten. Having gotten no response from either, she was determined to put the matter out of her mind once and for all. Discovering a sister she'd always wanted had been too good to be true.

So the e-mail with *Acorn Forest Apartments* as a subject, which she found in her inbox on July 7, was unexpected and got her attention. It read:

"I saw your request in the L. A. Times a while back and now, as it appeared again in the local paper, I assume that it is important. Roughly 40 years ago, I was a tenant in the apartment complex in San Remo you referred to but need more information before I can agree to your request.

"Basically, I would like to know the reason for your inquiry.

"Bob Tully"

Sherry sent a reply. She could not give him the real reason for looking into the past, but mentioned at least part of the truth by stating she'd lived in the apartments from birth until two years old. Her dad's comment came to mind, and she told a white lie of writing her memoir. In a follow-up e-mail correspondence they exchanged phone numbers and made a date to meet in person at a local Starbucks on Thursday at four o'clock in the afternoon.

On Thursday, after making introductions, they carried their drinks to a table at the Starbucks and settled themselves into chairs.

Sherry judged Bob Tully to be a man in his early to mid-sixties. He was lean, had a full head of dark, graying hair, and wore a dress shirt with rolled-up sleeves and stone-colored chinos. It soon became clear that Bob was chatty.

He started with, "So you're writing your memoir, but why are the first two years of your life important? What I mean is, you can't remember anything from that early on, so why go into details about the Acorn Forest Apartments?"

"Because my mom died there."

That shocked him. He first clasped a hand over his mouth and then exclaimed, "Oh no! You're the little girl whose mother drowned in the pool. I'm so sorry."

"You needn't be. I don't even remember her. But please tell me everything you recall about the Acorn Forest Apartments and its people during the time you lived there."

"Sure. I love to think back to when I was young," he remarked, and elaborated, "I was fresh out of school at the time and worked as an interior decorator, even though I'd studied interior design in college." He emphasized, "Yes, there is a difference. A designer is trained to create a first-rate interior space, while an interior decorator is more interested in making a place look attractive. It was easier to get hired by a company as a decorator since designers tend to be independent."

He went on, "The pay was lousy but I managed to scrape by with renting a one-bedroom apartment. My job was in Glendale, so the commute from San Remo wasn't bad. In those days, folks took surface streets to get to that neck of the woods. The Glendale Freeway connecting L. A. with the foothill communities was in its last stages of construction, and the section of the Foothill Freeway near San Remo had yet to be completed."

Sherry sipped her cappuccino, thinking, get to the point already!

As if he was reading her mind Bob said, "But you want to know all about the apartment complex. It was an extremely socially active community. During the day, especially in the summer, people gathered around the pool. The place was family oriented with mostly two- and three-bedroom apartments. The only building that had a few one-bedroom units was the one I lived in, right next to the pool area.

"Most adult tenants were married couples in their twenties and thirties and had children. They stayed a few years while saving up for a home of their own, or until they moved on to other towns. Besides swimming, there was plenty more for kids to do. There was a playground with swings, a slide, and other equipment, and a little track for riding bikes or tricycles. Every weekend, there seemed to have been a birthday party in one unit or another, judging from the balloons hanging from patios or balconies advertising the fact. And people had adult parties too, for all sorts of occasions. Halloween, New Year's, St. Patrick's Day, Fourth of July; you name it."

He took a sip of his caramel Frappuccino through the straw, then chuckled and recalled, "A lot of wife-husband swapping going on at that time in the place too."

"Really?"

"It seemed to be the fad in those days, shortly before the AIDS epidemic broke out in our country. As long as the birth control issue was taken care of, people felt safe."

Sherry asked, "Were you involved?"

"Oh, no. I'm gay. At the time, I was still 'in the closet,' but I had obviously no interest in any wife-swapping activities."

"So how did you know it was going on?"

"As I said, people were socially active in that apartment residence. I had joined a bridge club where we played cards every other Wednesday evening. My bridge partner, a divorced woman, was an excellent player and sharp. We even challenged each other to an occasional game of chess. She was also a gossip and knew everybody's business in the entire complex. She was the person who told me about the swapping."

Then Sherry inquired, "Did you know my family?"

"Not personally, but I knew who your parents were and I believe they had two kids, you and your brother. And from my balcony, I saw your mother often swimming laps in the evenings. My apartment was on the second floor, overlooking the pool."

With a catch in her throat she asked, "Did you see her on the night of the accident?"

"No, I came home late that night and had barely gone off to sleep when I was woken up after 2:00 a.m. by the commotion going on in the pool area where she was found."

They had finished their beverages and Sherry noticed that the place was getting crowded. She reflected on what more to ask when he said, "I'm curious, did other people answer your ad?"

"No, you're the only one, and I'm really thankful for your time and input."

"Sorry that I didn't know your mother better and can't help with giving you information about her."

"Speaking of other people, did you by chance keep in contact with any former tenants of the apartment complex?"

He replied, "Just one person, Gloria Morris, the bridge player lady I told you about. I love playing bridge and since she was also a fanatic about the game, we formed our own club after we both moved away from the apartments. We kept it up for decades and, until two years ago, she and I were bridge partners against two other people and met once a month. On occasion, the two of us also entered bridge tournaments."

"What happened two years ago?"

"One of the players passed away and my friend, who was 82 by then, moved to a retirement community. So the bridge club fell apart."

"But you still keep in touch with her?"

"Sure. I've been to visit her a few times."

Sherry said, "I'd like to talk with her."

Bob stated, "I won't give out her number without permission, but I'll get in touch with her and then let you know."

She thanked him again before getting up to leave. Once outside and ready to go their separate ways, he remarked, "I'm looking forward to reading your memoir."

"If it ever gets published," she replied. She then quickly turned away, bothered by a bad conscience, and walked to where her car was parked. Such a nice man, she thought, and I lied to him.

CHAPTER 12

It took Sherry a few days to gather the courage to tackle her dad again. On Monday morning, July 13, she waited until ten o'clock to make sure Vanessa had left for work and Dad was back from his daily walk before she arrived at his home in Arcadia.

He gave her a bear hug and chanted, "If I knew you were coming I'd have made cookies."

"You mean 'baked a cake,'" she said, amused. Then immediately became serious and announced, "We need to talk."

"I figured as much, since you came marching in unannounced. Let's go sit in the backyard before it gets too hot. Want something to drink?"

"No thanks, I had coffee for breakfast."

Max cranked up the large sun umbrella and they seated themselves on the cushioned patio chairs.

He said, "So you're not letting it rest."

"What do you mean?"

"I saw your ad in the paper. Did you get any responses?"

"Only one, from a man named Bob Tully. Do you remember him?"

"Not offhand."

"I had a chat with him last week. He lived at the Acorn Forest Apartments around the same time we did."

Her dad said, "Don't tell me you asked the man whether he had noticed a third kid belonging to our family."

"Certainly not. But Mr. Tully remembered some astonishing things going on in those apartments at that time." And she looked him square in the eye and said, "I want the truth, Dad. Were you and Mom involved in the wife/husband swapping business?"

Max's expression turned to shame and sadness as he nodded and said, "We were coaxed into that group of people. But don't confuse it with the hippies and flower children communal living, where they ingested LSD and everything was shared, even kids. It was nothing like that. Just recreational sex, no strings attached. The swapping was supposed to be all fun and games - - we were living the sexual revolution of the 70's - - but some jealousies and backstabbing occurred.

"Your mother and I knew that what we did was morally wrong. We did not stay in the group for long and got out of it way before you were born. I've always been ashamed and regretted those few weeks out of my life. I'm so sorry that you learned of it and are burdened with that knowledge now. Please forgive me."

Sherry ignored his plea and asked, "How many people were part of that group?"

"About a dozen."

"That's six different partners for each person," Sherry stated, and couldn't keep the disgust out of her voice.

After a long pause he said, "There were strict rules among the group. The most important was about protection. Emotional attachments or personal relationships were forbidden. I won't go into all those rules, but pregnancies resulting from the swapping were nearly impossible."

"Have you kept in touch with anyone of the group?"

"You must be joking. For years I've made it my business to forget those folks and what we participated in. Heck, I can't even remember their names. They were not bad people, just misguided and young. We were all young and dumb."

And after another long silence he said, "Poker - - I mean Sherry - - you and I have always had a good father/daughter relationship. I hope it's not ruined because of the stupid immoral thing I did four decades ago."

"I'll try to forget about it."

"Please don't tell Ben. He tends to be judgmental."

"I hadn't planned on telling him."

"And put the absurd idea about having a sister out of your head."

She was trying not to be judgmental herself and, ready to leave, asked one last question. "What was the argument about?"

"What argument?"

"You told me that on the night of Mom's drowning, she stormed out to the pool because the two of you were arguing. So what was the fight about?"

"I have no idea," he replied. "Do you expect me to remember after all this time?" And he hoped that his eyes did not belie his words.

CHAPTER 13

Max had a restless night. Thanks to his daughter, all the anguish that had plagued him for many years after Emma's drowning was back with a vengeance. Instead of drifting off to sleep, the terrifying image of seeing her motionless at the bottom of the pool forced itself back into his mind again, as if it had happened yesterday. He re-lived diving into the pool, pulling her to the surface, and attempting mouth-to-mouth, knowing there was no chance of success.

They had pulled out of the swapping group more than two and a half years before his wife's drowning accident, and the four of them had lived a happy family life, but something had been lost between Emma and him, never to be the same. The moral issue had weighed much heavier on her than it had affected him. He had not realized it until the damage was done. Like he'd told Poker, it was all supposed to have been fun and games to lighten up the monotony of married life. But in Emma's case, it had backfired. He blamed himself for what had happened.

Had there been a different ending to their argument that night, his wife would still be alive.

Margit, the nanny, turned out to be a great help, especially during the first few months when he had difficulty coping. After she returned to Norway, he had done the best he could to bring up the kids by himself, and there had been a special bond between him and Sherry. Was that ruined now with her knowledge of his past sin? Agitated, he tossed in bed, trying to finally erase his fixation of long-ago events and get some rest.

Vanessa touched his arm gently and asked, "Can't sleep? What's bothering you?"

"Images from the past. Never mind me."

Easy for him to say after he woke me up with his trashing around, she thought. Unlike him, I have to go to work in the morning rather than sleeping in. And she was already starting to drift off again as she mused, serves me right for getting involved with a man who seems to have a lot of baggage.

****

Sherry, for her part, was afflicted with a nightmare of her own that same night. She saw a woman being hit over the head with a baseball bat, then thrown into a pool. There was a gurgling sound and bubbles forming in the water as the woman sank to the bottom in slow motion. Sherry wanted to jump to the rescue, but could not move as someone held her back.

She woke with a scream and sat up straight in bed.

"What's the matter?" Dave asked.

"Just a dream," she said, "go back to sleep." Which he immediately did.

For Sherry, sleep did not come again for a long time. Granted, it was only a nightmare, but it would not leave her alone. What if Mom's drowning was not an accident but she was killed? Impossible! Who would want to harm her? Besides, according to Dad, the medical examiner had ruled that her head wound was caused by crashing into the pool's edge when doing a turnaround while swimming laps. There must have been concrete evidence of this for the coroner to have reached those findings. But the image of someone knocking her mom unconscious and then throwing her into the pool would not leave her any peace of mind.

Forget about it, she told herself. It was a bad dream and had nothing to do with reality. All of a sudden, she wished that she had never started digging up the past. So she had a Doppelgänger, big deal. If back in Hawaii she had used the bathroom in their own hotel room instead of the one near the lobby, she'd have never met Kirsten. No doubt, she would be leading a happy life now, not knowing of the other's existence. And she would have been spared finding out about Dad and Mom joining that disgusting group in the apartment complex.

Well, she decided, it will end right now. I don't have a sister; it was all in my imagination. Like Dad suggested, I will put the absurd idea out of my mind and go on with my life! That settled, she finally got back to sleep.

When Dave entered the kitchen on Tuesday morning, he found Sherry there already, scrambling eggs and humming a tune to herself.

"You're up early and in a chipper mood," he remarked.

"That's right. I've made the decision to drop the whole Kirsten thing. I was in a fantasy world thinking that we could be related. She is nothing but some stranger who happens to look like me. The woman must have thought I was a nutcase when reading my letter and didn't think it deserved an answer. Well, I've come to my senses now."

"Good for you!"

"And what's more, I'm done spending my entire summer chasing after something that doesn't exist. Summer school is in session, so as soon as the office opens this morning, I'll call and let the administrator know that I'm available for tutoring."

She went on, "And maybe we can plan a little road trip to Northern California toward the end of the month. You have some more vacation time coming. We might as well make the best of it."

"That's my Sherry. Welcome back!" Dave said, digging into his breakfast with gusto.

CHAPTER 14

Rather than getting in touch via phone - - as the woman refused to wear a hearing aid - - Bob Tully decided to see Gloria Morris, his former bridge partner, in person. A visit to her was overdue, and he had time since the event planning business was in a summer lull.

On Wednesday afternoon, July 15, he signed himself in at the reception desk, and then found her in the recreation hall of the retirement community's main building, bent over a jigsaw puzzle. He had to call out her name twice before she looked up.

"Bobby!" she shouted, "what a nice surprise!" She scrambled to her feet and said, "Let me get you something to drink from the refreshment counter."

Seeing that there were plenty of folks around, he stopped her and said, "I'd prefer sitting outside, where we have more privacy."

"Oh, by all means, if it's privacy that you want," she hollered, and winked at him. "The AC in here is set too low for my liking anyways."

She took off her cardigan, hung it over the backrest of the chair, and they slowly made their way to the establishment's garden, where they found a bench in the shade of a Juniper tree.

He asked, "Do you enjoy living in this place now?"

"I've gotten used to it. Not having to do my own cooking and cleaning is a plus, and I've made some friends, even though I still hate being around so many old folks. Some talk about nothing but their ailments, which is boring like hell. I've met a man who's a decent chess player, though. I'd introduce you, but he's in the hospital getting a knee replacement."

Then Gloria looked him in the eye and said, "So, tell me all about *your* life since last time we spoke. Did you resolve the little issue you had with Ralph?"

"Oh, sure. It wasn't really a big deal after all."

"And did you find your cat?"

"Yes, Snicker came home the very next day."

"What's that?"

He yelled, "We have Snicker back!" and reminded himself to speak louder.

"What about that reunion party you were so stressed about, did that end up going smoothly?"

Bob had to think back, trying to remember what she was talking about, and then answered in the affirmative. He thought, she may be hard of hearing and have some arthritis in her hips, but her mind is as sharp as ever.

He said, "Do you remember our days in the Acorn Forest Apartments?"

"You good and well know that I do. In fact, I have fond memories of the place, especially our bridge club."

He stated, "You personally knew a lot of residents and their secrets."

She tittered and said, "You mean I was a busybody. And you're right, I did enjoy ferreting out all about people." She pointed a finger at him, saying, "Out with it, why are you bringing this up now?"

He told her about the ad in the paper and his meeting with Sherry. She heard him out and then said, "The drowning of Emma Andino was tragic, indeed."

"You still remember her full name," Bob remarked. "I don't think I ever knew it."

"So why is Sherry interested in the past? I mean, if it's about her mother, why wait this long before inquiring?"

"She's writing her memoir."

"Oh, then it actually makes sense."

Bob said, "She wanted to know about people and life in general in the apartment complex. I couldn't tell her much but did mention the wife/husband swapping that went on at the time we lived there."

"I see."

With an embarrassed grin he said, "By the way, I always wondered, were you active in the swapping?"

"Good grief, no! It strictly involved couples. I was at least a decade older than the people in that group and a single mother with a teenage son at that. Besides, no matter what, it wouldn't have been my thing. And you, Bobby, were hardly more than a child."

"I was 22 when I moved into the apartment!"

"Like I said, a baby!"

Their conversation came to a halt as a couple walked by, humming a tune in harmony. The man was supported by a cane, and the woman held a parasol. They nodded a greeting and made eye contact, never missing a beat in their harmonizing.

"What a cheerful pair," Bob remarked.

"They're excellent musicians. Every so often they give a concert in the recreation hall."

Then he said, "Coming back to our subject, Sherry wanted to know if I kept in touch with other former tenants of the Acorn Forest Apartments - - -"

"And you mentioned me," she finished his sentence. "I know you thought I was a gossip, and that was true, but when it came to serious transgressions, I kept my tongue."

"And there were some of those?"

"Plenty, but don't try to get me to reveal old sins." She giggled and said, "You can read them all in my diary after I've passed away."

"Are you still in contact with other former renters that Sherry could talk to?"

"There's Karl and Peggy - - I don't know if you remember them - - but they won't be any use to her. Peggy is dying of cancer and Karl is senile. Time catches up with us one way or another. I don't know which is worse, the physical deterioration or the mental."

"Would you consider talking with Sherry, and if so, may I give her your number?"

"Sure. It will be interesting to see what kind of woman she has become. I saw her last when she was only two years old. But my chat with her will have to wait for a while as my son and daughter-in-law are taking me on an Alaskan cruise. We leave this Friday."

"You had better start packing, then!"

CHAPTER 15

Over a week later, on Thursday, July 23 to be exact, Kirsten sat in the office section of her den. She reached into the top desk drawer to grab a few of her business cards for restocking folders and noticed Sherry's letter she had forgotten all about. As she reread it now, it became clear that the woman was serious about her exploration, even desperate, it seemed. She decided to answer the letter. It would be rude not to. Also, her response would make it clear to her lookalike that they were not related, and that would be the end of their communication. Sharing her marital status, kids, profession, and hobbies was easy enough. She wasn't sure about the rest, though, and first needed to get in touch with her parents for answers.

Kirsten started dialing their land line and then changed her mind, never knowing what kind of mood she would find her mother in. She checked the time. It was 1:20 in the afternoon. Her appointment to show a house nearby was not until 1:45, and Dad should be in recess right now. So she rang his cell phone.

****

On that Thursday afternoon, Judge Ericson, one of the presiding judges of the United States District Court, was returning to the Federal Courthouse in Orange County from his lunch recess. The court would resume its session at 2 o'clock, but he had ordered both the defense counselor and the prosecutor for a discussion in his chamber at 1:30. They had each taken liberties with misleading the jury in the current trial and he needed to set them straight.

The present case was a particular grueling one. On days like this, he wondered if he should start thinking about retirement. At 67, he was in good health and in possession of all his faculties, but maybe it was time to hang up the robe. His wife, Louise, was a few years older and had retired from her job as a social worker a long time ago. In later years, she suffered from depression. He had no idea what brought it on, but her condition was hard for them both to live with.

He owed a lot to Louise. She'd financially supported him through law school, and thanks to her parents, they had been able to buy their first house. Even back then, years before the onset of her condition, Louise had been unpredictable and any attempt of his to figure out what went on in her mind was useless.

He had come a long way since those law school days, having made his own mark on a life of success, first as a DA, and now as a federal judge, a position he had been appointed to a couple of decades ago. But he never forgot that Louise had helped start it all. And she was the mother of pampered Kirsten, their only child.

He nodded to himself, it was possible that retirement would make a difference. They could take long trips and go on cruises. Maybe if he could give her his full attention, she would get better. They could play golf together and go for long walks with Ember, their Schnauzer, if Louise was willing.

After mulling this over, he was about to look at his notes to go over with the attorneys when his phone chimed.

He glanced at the number, took the call, and said, "Kirsten! What a pleasant surprise."

"Hi Dad. Do you have a minute or two?"

"For you, always."

"First off, how is Mom doing?"

"She started a new medication and we hope it will help. Are we going to get to see you and your family soon?"

"We're pretty busy right now; perhaps next month. I have a couple questions. What was the small town near Pasadena we lived in called before we moved to Orange County? I started Kindergarten soon after the move, so I must have been close to five. I remember a big apartment complex, but can't recall the place."

"That was the Acorn Forest Apartments in San Remo."

"Right, San Remo. That sounds familiar. And you're of Scandinavian descent. What about Mom, does she have relatives of Greek background?"

The judge laughed out loud. "Greek? What a funny question. As far as I know, your mother comes from German, Austrian, and possibly a bit of Dutch lineage. What's this interrogation about?"

Kirsten told him about her encounter with Sherry in Hawaii and then read the letter out aloud.

He listened and then stated, "People resembling one another is common and means nothing. You are not related to this woman. It is obvious that she wants to strike up a friendship with you on the mere premise that you two look alike. Don't answer the letter. She sounds a bit unstable."

The two attorneys arrived at that moment and he said, "I have to go. Say hi to Mike and the kids, and come visit us soon."

"I promise."

As they ended the call Kirsten thought, first Mike told me to ignore Sherry's request and now Dad said so too. I feel like I did as a child; the more grownups told me not to do something, the more I wanted to do it. I *will* answer the letter but it can wait until another day; right now I'm off to show my new client a bargain of a house.

CHAPTER 16

At their home in Irvine, the Judge looked at Louise sitting across from him at the dinner table. They had finished their meal of baked salmon with rice pilaf and asparagus, and now lingered over a cup of coffee. The pair could well afford a cook in addition to their housekeeper, but Louise insisted on preparing meals herself. There were times when her illness made her too withdrawn for the task. On those occasions, he either managed meals on his own or ate out. On that particular evening, however, he found her in good spirits and tending to supper when he got home.

He said, "Kirsten called me today. They're coming for a visit soon."

"Really? She called you at work to tell you *that*?"

He had hoped that the news would please her but now wished he hadn't mentioned the call.

"As a matter of fact, she also wanted some information."

"About what?"

He had no choice now but to go into what he had learned. With Louise, he never knew how she would react. So he told her about Kirsten's Doppelgänger and the letter she had received. He added that he thought it strange that the woman wanted to know what town their daughter had lived in at an early age, and found the bit about the ancestry even stranger.

She took it in her stride and remarked, "How bizarre!" And then her mood changed and she added, "I never liked the place."

"San Remo?"

"No, not the little town with its old-world charm. I meant the apartment complex we lived in."

"It served a purpose while you supported me through law school." He smirked and remarked, "But you have to admit, we had some fun times there, socializing with neighbors, being invited to parties and barbecues, and mingling with people around the pool area. Best of all, there were lots of little playmates for Kirsten."

She refrained from commenting and he felt her sudden detachment. Like always when this happened, he was powerless. The long silence between them was nerve-racking for him, but she seemed unaware of it.

He was about to get up and walk away when she said, "What was her last name?"

"Huh?"

"The Sherry woman. You told me that Kirsten read you the entire letter, and that it was signed with her current and also her maiden name."

"I believe it was something like Undino-Rinaldi."

"You mean *Andino?*"

"That's it."

Louise stated, "So we lived in the same apartment complex. What a coincidence! That makes her Emma Andino's daughter."

"And who is she?"

"You honestly don't remember?"

He shook his head.

"Emma is the woman who drowned in the apartment pool."

"Of course, I remember the tragic drowning accident - - I'm sure everyone does who lived there at that time - - but forgot her name."

"She was in that group of people you persuaded me to join."

"You mean the swapping couples?"

She winced and said, "I hated that term then, and it sounds even worse now, but I guess that's what we were."

"As I recall, it started out as nothing more than a bit of fun until some of us got jealous."

"Don't beat around the bush. I was the one getting jealous, and with good reason. I wasn't cut out to be in that kind of an environment."

"Exactly," he agreed. "That's why we didn't participate in those activities for long and left the group."

After another stretch of silence where Louise was in her own world and far from reach, she suddenly snapped out of it and asked, "So what's happening now? Is Kirsten going to pursue this by answering Sherry?"

"I advised her not to."

"Which doesn't mean that she won't. Our Kirsten has a mind of her own."

"You're right on that account."

Earlier, on his drive home, Judge Ericson had intended to discuss his possible retirement with his wife but changed his mind. For now, one revelation had been enough to burden her with. He went to the hallway, grabbed Ember's leash from its hook, and took the Schnauzer for a short after-dinner walk.

CHAPTER 17

Ben, Sherry's brother, called her on Saturday morning, July 25. Before he could get a word in edgewise she said, "I was about to get in touch with you to let you know that Dave and I are going to be out of town for a week, starting Tuesday."

"Where to?"

"Just a road trip to Northern California for a change of scenery. We might get in a hike or two."

"Sounds great. The reason I'm calling, I dug up two photos of our mom. Do you want them?"

"Sure, I'd like to see them but there's no hurry. I've dropped the - -" she was searching for a word "- - project since our last phone call."

Angry now, he said, "If I've wasted my time going through old stuff to find those pictures, you can at least tell me what this project of yours was about."

"It's a long story," she said, "which I'll tell you someday. But I'm still curious, what were her hair and eye color?"

"I'm looking at one of the photos. Her hair was brown and so were her eyes. The last time we talked, you asked about some kid's hair color. What's all this fascination with hair and eye coloring?"

"Has it ever occurred to you that I'm the only fair person in our family? Everyone else is dark haired."

"Are you saying that you think you're adopted?"

She hesitated for a second and then decided to let him assume so. She said, "It's not that farfetched. Aside from the coloring, I don't look remotely like anyone else in the family."

"Yes, it is farfetched! Lots of kids don't look like their parents or siblings. It doesn't mean a thing. And now that I'm thinking back and picturing people, grandma on our mother's side was blonde."

"That's debatable. She may have dyed her hair, which can't be proven either way since she's long dead."

Ben said, "I can't believe we're having this conversation. You're my blood sister and that's that. I'm glad you dropped your so-called project."

They changed the subject and briefly talked about Ben's upcoming camping trip with his family in August, and then wished each other bon voyage for their respective trips.

CHAPTER 18

In late afternoon on Monday of the last week in July, Sherry was all packed for the trip when the high school student she was tutoring in French finally arrived at her house.

He said, "Sorry I'm late. Had to find somebody to jump-start my wheels first."

"Well, you're here now. Let's make the best of it."

They seated themselves in the den, where the student opened his workbook.

Sherry said, "Before we look at the sentences I gave you to translate at our last session, I want to make sure you understand the usage of auxiliary verbs." She looked at him and added, "Which are?"

"I think *être* and *avoir*," he said.

"Meaning?"

"To be and to have."

"Correct. An easy way to determine which regular verbs take *être* and which take *avoir* is by their ending.

Regular verbs ending in 'er' are conjugated with *être*, and the ones ending in 'ir' are conjugated with *avoir*. For example, the verb *arriver* in the perfect tense is conjugated, *je suis arrivé, tu es arrivé,*" and she proceeded to conjugate the verb in its entirety.

She went on, "In comparison, the verb *finir* amounts to, *j'ai fini, tu as fini,*" and she continued down the line, conjugating each personal pronoun with the correct verb and its ending.

He nodded, but she wasn't sure whether he fully understood and said, "You know, of course, what the verb *finir* translates to, right?"

"Sure, it means to finish."

"Correct. And if you'd use *être* with it instead of *avoir*, saying '*je suis fini*', what would that mean?"

She had lost him for sure now as he said, "That it's wrong?"

"Actually, it changes the meaning. '*Je suis fini*' means 'I am dead.'"

And she said, "Now let's see those sentences I gave you for homework."

To her pleasant surprise, his translation from English to French read well. There were a couple of places where he had mixed up the gender of a noun and consequently used the wrong articles and word-endings but, overall, he had done good work. So the two previous lessons she had covered with him had made a difference. As a teacher, that knowledge gave her satisfaction.

On the other hand, one of the short phrases put her on edge all over again. She must have had a one-track mind when giving him, "What a nightmare!" to translate. He had correctly turned it into French with, "*Quel cauchemar!*" In an instant, the horrific dream of the other night, where she watched a woman drown, was back in her head. She shook the image free from her mind and praised the student for a job well done.

Then she said, "What we cover for the rest of today's lesson is your choice. We can go over some more grammar or converse a bit in French."

He opted for the latter, and although his pronunciation was a bit off, he was able to communicate with simple expressions. Time passed quickly and as he got up to leave, he said, "See you next week."

"Make that the following week. Starting tomorrow, I'm going to be out of town for a while."

"*Amusez-vous bien!*" he said and left.

Only a minute later he rang her doorbell once more, and when she answered it, he begged, "I need your help with jump-starting my car."

"I don't think we have any cables and I don't know how to do that."

"I have them and know how."

Sherry looked toward the street where his older-model Chevy was parked and said, "Go ahead. If there's any noise involved, I'm sure the neighbors will understand."

He stared at her and thought, how can a smart woman be so dumb? Aloud he said, "It needs a second car."

"Oh, I see," she said, grabbed her keys, and went to drive her own vehicle out of the garage. Following the boy's instructions, she then parked it on the street facing the Chevrolet. The student knew what to do. In fact, he seemed to be an expert.

When he had his engine running she said, "I think you need to purchase a new battery."

"Or keep the starter cables handy," he said with a grin and took off.

Sherry watched as the Chevy made its way down her street, then turned right at the stop, barely slowing down. She shook her head. Could it be that the student jump-started his car every time he drove it instead of investing in a new battery?

CHAPTER 19

The journey to Lake Tahoe was about a nine-hour drive, so they left their house in Pasadena at 7:30 a.m. They took turns driving, with Dave taking the first stretch. The ride north on Interstate 5 was boring, especially in mid-summer when the landscape was ugly brown and dried out.

Yawning, Sherry remarked, "I got up way too early." She closed her eyes and dozed, on and off. The feedlot at Harris Ranch made her come to her senses, first by the smell and then the impressive view. The ranch, a San Joaquin Valley landmark halfway between Los Angeles and Sacramento, raised the finest beef on the West coast. They lunched at Harris Ranch Restaurant and enjoyed their Cajun beef tips.

Following their lunch stop, it was Sherry's turn behind the wheel. They soon left the open field of ranch cattle behind and drove along orchards of pistachio and almond trees for miles. For the most part, though, the scenery along I-5 was monotonous, so they listened to classic rock to keep alert.

When Sherry was driving through Sacramento, merging onto I-80, Dave offered to stop someplace and take over again, but she preferred to keep going. She would rather concentrate on driving than be left to musing. After passing the town of Auburn, the road climbed steadily toward the Donner Pass.

Dave pointed and said, "Remember Sugar Bowl?"

"Sure do. We skied it three years ago."

"There are trails from there to Donner Peak and Mt. Judah. Let's drive back during our stay in Tahoe and do those hikes."

They arrived in Tahoe City shortly after 4:30, where they had hotel reservations, with plenty of time to unpack and freshen up before heading out on the town for a stroll and dinner.

****

Over the next few days the couple took advantage of the many activities charming Tahoe City offered. On Wednesday they rented paddleboards and kayaks to explore the deep-blue waters of Lake Tahoe's West shore. The next day they hiked the trail to Eagle Falls and Eagle Lake. The views down to the lake were breathtaking and they paired the hike with a walk down to Emerald Bay.

On Friday, they opted for an excursion to Truckee, a 35-minute drive from North Shore Lake Tahoe. The deep-rooted railroad town took them back to the times of pioneers as they toured the old jail, the Red Light district, the Chinese herb shop, and the depot. There were plenty of restaurants with delicious food. Sherry, in particular, enjoyed window shopping in historic downtown Truckee.

There was something for everyone: clothes, jewelry, art, furniture, and kitchen gadgets.

The two spent the weekend relaxing in town and on the beach. It wasn't until Monday, August 3, that they finally ventured down the highway to Sugar Bowl to hike the Donner and Judah Peaks. They parked along the road near the Sugar Bowl Academy and picked up the trailhead to the Pacific Crest Trail. The track started out with the most difficult stretch, a series of rocky switchbacks. Once they had reached the top of the switchbacks, the trail changed into a long, winding uphill climb through a pine forest.

About a mile up, they got to the junction of trails. A sharp left turn would have led them to Donner Peak but they chose the Judah loop and continued on the trail to the right. After another mile of steadily ascending through woodland, the trail turned east and they climbed the last stretch through the trees to the summit of Mt. Judah.

Slightly out of breath, Sherry stood at the crest with both arms extended toward the sky and called out, "This is heaven! It makes me realize how little my troubles matter."

"You have troubles?" Dave asked with a mocking grin.

Then he draped an arm around her shoulders and drew her close, remarking, "The view from here makes the hike well worth the effort," and pointing south, he added, "There's the Anderson Peak and the Granite Chief Wilderness." Directing her to the north, he said, "Look across Donner Pass. The turret-shaped summit is Castle Peak."

"And there's the Sugar Bowl ski area," Sherry said, pointing straight down. "Let's ski that again next winter."

After enjoying the 360-degree panorama, they descended the ridge line. Farther downhill, where the trail reunited with the one leading to Donner Peak, Dave asked, "Want to climb up to Donner Peak now?"

Sherry shook her head. "My legs have had enough of a workout." And so they returned down the mountain to the trailhead.

On Tuesday, their last day of vacation, they drove the short distance to Kings Beach at the California/Nevada Stateline. Although the Casinos there were not as elaborate as the ones at the South Shore, they enjoyed spending time at the blackjack tables and shooting craps. When they called it quits in the evening, Dave was ahead by a few dollars and Sherry had come out even. Checking her phone when she got back to the hotel, Sherry saw the new e-mail message.

A loud shriek escaped her as she read it.

Dave asked, "Something wrong?"

She did not answer him but read the message again:

"Hi Sherry,

"As you listed two numbers in your letter, I dialed them both and got an answering machine when I called the landline, and your cell phone went into voicemail. I did not leave a message on either but decided to send this e-mail instead.

"To set your mind at ease that we are not related, here's some personal info about me. San Remo was the small town where I lived the first five years of my life in an apartment complex called Acorn Forest. As far as ancestry, my father has a full-fledged Scandinavian background, and my mother is of

German, Austrian, and Dutch origin. So you see, there's no Greek anywhere!

"To your other questions. I'm 43 years old and you apparently know that I'm married. We have two children, a boy of 13 and a girl of 11, and I'm a real estate agent. I don't have any hobbies since I'm too busy with work and family life.

"Have a good day,

"Kirsten Ericson-Hiller"

"PS: How did you know that I am married and where did you get my address?"

Sherry recovered from the initial shock, handed him the phone and said, "We lived in the same apartments at the same time! That can't be a coincidence."

Dave read the message and had to agree that brushing it off as a mere coincidence would not do, but inwardly he cringed. This meant that Sherry would pursue her hunt anew. He had been so relieved during the entire trip that she was being her normal, cheerful self again. Their days had been full of adventures and appreciation of nature, and there had been plenty of friendliness at night. Now, that e-mail message would tip the scale, and she'd throw herself full force into her quest once more.

He said, "You have a point but there is still the possibility that your strong resemblance to this woman is nothing but a fluke. So don't jump to conclusions."

"Don't worry, I'm not! I'll find out the truth, once and for all. We'll have to have our DNA analyzed and compared."

At dawn the next morning, they started on their drive home via Reno, for a change of scenery. They bypassed the

Mammoth region and made their lunch stop in Bishop. Although the landscape had more to offer than the one on their ride up on I-5, Sherry hardly noticed. Her mind was on the e-mail message she had received the night before.

CHAPTER 20

It was back to work for Dave on Thursday and Sherry took care of chores that had accumulated while they had been away. She tended to laundry, sorted through the mail, paid bills, and watered the rose bushes in their yard. She did all that like a robot while her brain concentrated on how to proceed, now that she knew of her definite link to Kirsten.

She put a second load into the washing machine and thought, how do I break the news to unsuspecting Kirsten? Full speed ahead was the best policy. No more pussyfooting around. The woman deserved to learn the truth as much as she herself did. They needed to get their DNA tested and get proof, one way or another.

Sherry took out her cell phone and scrolled for Kirsten's number on the "missed call" notice she'd received while in Tahoe, and dialed it.

****

Kirsten was about to leave her home to put up a real estate stake sign at the front yard of a new property, when she received the call. She checked the number and thought, I have nothing more to say, but answered it.

"Hi Kirsten," Sherry said, "Thanks for your e-mail. Before I forget, I knew that you were married because the man at the concierge desk at the hotel called you Mrs. Hiller. Getting your address was easy. You told me your first name and that you lived in San Diego, so finding a Kirsten Hiller there was a piece of cake. But that's not why I'm calling. Prepare yourself for some astonishing news."

Kirsten checked the time and thought, get on with it already. Sherry continued, "You mentioned that you are 43 years old and that you lived at the Acorn Forest Apartments in San Remo for the first five years of your life. I'm 42 and lived there for the first two years of mine."

There was a slight pause while Kirsten took it in and then burst out, "What an odd coincidence!"

"I'll say. We look exactly alike and lived in the same place at the same time."

"What are you hinting at?"

"We may be sisters, half-sisters, or otherwise blood related."

"Are you suggesting that one of us is adopted?"

"That's one possibility but I don't think so."

Annoyed, Kirsten asked, "What are you implying? Be straight with me."

Sherry had anticipated this and knew there was no way around it. So she told her about the swapping that had gone on in that apartment complex before she was born.

"How do you know this?" Kirsten asked.

"It's a long story. Do you have time?"

"Not really, but tell me anyway."

So Sherry explained how she found Bob Tully and what she learned from him. She also told her about her mom's drowning accident, without going into details.

Kirsten said, "You are suggesting that our parents were involved in this wife/husband swapping thing, but you really don't know. Or do you?"

"I questioned my dad about it and he admitted that he and my mom had belonged to the group. I don't know if you want to grill your folks, but you may not have to."

"What do you mean?"

Sherry stated, "The surest way to find out if we're blood related is to have our DNA tested."

"You're kidding."

"I'm dead serious. It can be done through one of those heritage sites that are advertised. I'll do a bit of research and then get back to you."

On that note they ended the call.

Minutes later, Kirsten lifted the stake sign into the trunk of her car and was off to run her errand. However, her mind was far from her job. She was trying to process what she'd just learned. All of it was a great shock. The bit that her parents could have been involved in what was going on in those apartments, made her shudder. And the idea of questioning them about it was something she could not imagine doing. From Mom she would get nothing but an absent-minded stare. And Dad would be insulted at the query, and she doubted that he would deem it worth an answer.

Well, as Sherry had worded it, she could be spared the grilling of her parents by DNA testing. Could it really be that she was not the only child her parents had made her believe and that Sherry was her sister?

Two days later, the women each sent their mouth swabs to an ancestry company Sherry had researched, called peckingline.com, to determine whether their DNA was a sibling match.

CHAPTER 21

Meanwhile, Louise Ericson sat underneath a sun umbrella in the back patio of her home in Irvine while the housekeeper was cleaning the inside of the house. She was holding an old photo album but was not looking through its pages. Instead, she stared, unseeing, straight ahead at their garden.

Why was life so complicated? she mused. Her quality of life had improved in the last few weeks due to a new medication she was taking. But now, knowing of the letter Kirsten had received from Sherry Andino, the past was catching up with her once again. For decades she had been able to shake it from her mind by immersing herself wholeheartedly into social work. That changed with her retirement, where she had plenty of time for brooding.

She knew her daughter well enough to be certain the letter would not go unanswered and the matter would be pursued. The Judge - - she had always called him that ever since his appointment - - had thought her oblivious to her surrounding in his law school days. But she had kept her eyes open even though it hurt. Back then, she had made her choice. Now, she tended to retreat into a world of her own instead of facing the music.

She now leafed through the photo album. There were many pictures of Kirsten as a baby, toddler, and her school years, some family shots of the three of them, and a few group pictures with friends. She was looking at photos taken during the few years they lived in the Acorn Forest Apartments. On one of the pages there was an empty space where it was evident that a photo had been removed. She stared at the gap. An image of herself surfaced where she had pulled the picture out of the album and torn it to pieces. This was some 40 years ago, but she remembered the photo in detail; a group of adults with their young children, gathered at the pool area.

She reflected on the four decades since then. After the move to their first house in Orange County, life had been good. All her energy and joy had gone into bringing up Kirsten and her job as social worker. Later, when their daughter was an adult and had been living on her own, they had given little Vinny a good home for a few years, which had made her feel much needed.

The housekeeper stuck her head out the patio's sliding glass door and called to her, "I'm done. See you next week, Mrs. Ericson."

Louise waved to her and checked the time. She should go inside and start thinking about what to cook for dinner. Then her eyes glanced back down to the empty spot in the album. Funny, the Judge had never questioned what had happened to the missing picture, yet he must have noticed its absence a long time ago.

On that evening, out of the blue, Louise asked her husband, "There is no statute of limitations on murder. Right?"

The Judge replied, "Correct. Why do you ask?"

"Just wondering."

He pinned her with a look full of scrutiny, but she said no more. It took him a second to realize that his wife was already out of reach.

CHAPTER 22

On Monday August 10, Bob Tully called Sherry, giving her Gloria Morris's number.

He said, "Gloria will be happy to talk with you. I saw her right before she went on a cruise, so I waited with telling you until now, as she is expected to be back. I hope you're still interested in getting in touch with her."

"I sure am," she said and thanked him.

Actually, Sherry had forgotten all about that other former tenant of the apartments but was now glad she had a new focus while waiting for those DNA tests to come back. She had to admit to herself that the wait made her antsy. When she got a hold of Gloria, the lady said she'd caught a cold during the Alaskan cruise and still felt a bit under the weather. She asked to be given another week or so to recover. Sherry made an appointment to see her on Thursday, August 20.

She got another call, this one from Dad, who invited her and Dave to a barbecue at his house on Sunday afternoon, August 16.

After checking her calendar Sherry said, "Sure, we'd love to come. Who else is invited?"

"Just your brother and family. Vanessa and I decided to have you all over before their camping trip, since summer will be coming to an end after they get back."

"By the way, Dad, I made an appointment to chat with Gloria Morris. Does she ring a bell?"

"No. Who is she?"

"A former tenant of the Acorn Forest Apartments."

"Gloria Morris," he repeated, letting the name sink in. Then he said, "I have a vague recollection of a woman by that name. She was older, either widowed or divorced, and known as a gossip throughout the place. I may have the name wrong, and the person you mentioned is someone else." And in the same breath he said, "I thought you've given up the 'looking for a sister' thing."

"Before our trip to Tahoe I'd dropped it but now it's back. I'm in contact with Kirsten, my double, and we've discovered that we lived in that apartment complex in San Remo at the same time!"

An involuntary sigh escaped Max but his daughter did not hear it, as she was preoccupied with a thought of her own. She remembered that Kirsten had included her maiden name when signing the e-mail.

She said, "Hold on a sec," and checked the e-mail message on her phone, then continued, "Did you know people by the name of Ericson when we lived there?"

"Sounds familiar but I can't put faces to the name. We're talking some 40 years ago. Why?"

"That was her name, Kirsten Ericson."

"According to you, she was a toddler at the time, but I don't remember the little girl."

"You must have known her parents."

"Maybe, but I don't recall." And he was irritated as he stated, "I know where this is going and don't like it. So by some strange coincidence you two lived in the same place and also happen to look alike. That does not make you sisters by a long shot. Do you realize how unreasonable this whole thing is? It has become an unhealthy obsession with you. Give it up for your own good, and everyone else's around you."

Aware that she had made him angry, she kept quiet about the DNA samples that were being tested that very moment.

CHAPTER 23

At lunchtime on August 11, a person sat before a full plate of food, contemplating the options. It was unfortunate that sins of the past were being dragged to the surface and possibly exposed. The person was confident, though, that it would never come to a trial after all those years. And if, against all odds, the case would end up in court after all, a jury would never convict. There were no witnesses, and there was no evidence of foul play. Still, it was important to avoid a trial. In other words, there could be no suspicion of murder where the drowning accident of Emma was concerned.

There was one individual, a woman, who had known - - or maybe only guessed - - and could be a threat. She needed to be silenced now. I should have taken care of her all those years ago, but it didn't seem necessary at the time, the culprit thought, figuring the busybody would have died by now. It turned out that she was still around. Well, that needed to be taken care of, but by someone else.

Minutes later, a phone call took place.

The caller said, "I have a pressing job for you. Do you understand what I'm talking about?"

The ex-hitman replied, "I don't take those jobs no more."

"I know, but this is important and you owe me a favor."

There was no answer.

"I'll make it worth your while. Let me tell you the details."

There was a grunt from the other end, and then, "Not on the phone. Meet me in your neighborhood park same time tomorrow," and the line went dead.

The person uttered a sigh of relief in anticipation of eliminating a possible liability. For a brief moment a pang of guilt crept into their mind but was shrugged off by a stronger survival instinct. The individual was now able to eat lunch before making a trip to the bank to withdraw a large amount of cash.

The next day, a man sat down two feet apart from the person already sitting on a secluded park bench. Both looked straight ahead, avoiding eye contact.

The newcomer said, "I'm clean and have quit that kind of business for good. I work legit now."

"I know and expected as much, but I'm desperate," the other said, adding, "How is Junior?"

"He's fine. I'll take the job because I owe you. And you're in luck, I'm officially on vacation. Don't tell me why you want it done. It is better if I don't know. Just give me the target's profile."

That barely took a couple minutes, and when accomplished, the former said, "Make it look like an accident; nothing else is acceptable."

There remained the matter of payment; half was due right away, and the rest upon completion of the job.

The neighborhood park was not crowded, and any casual observer would have missed the fact that one person had brought a bag along and the other had left with it.

CHAPTER 24

The two women each received their DNA results from peckingline.com on Friday of that week. Sherry immediately called Kirsten and exclaimed, "Hi there, Sis!"

Kirsten said, "I'm bowled over! There's no doubt about it. 75% certainty that we're sisters and 90% that we're half-sisters. We are blood-related for a fact." And she added, "I didn't expect it but believe that you did."

Sherry admitted, "I sure did and can't wait to get together and give you a big hug!"

They were both ecstatic and their conversation continued full of upbeat excitement for the first few moments until Kirsten's mood turned somber. She said, "We both know what that means."

"Yes, I've been trying to come to grips with it."

"So what do we do now?"

"We need to know who parented who."

There was a long pause and Sherry began to wonder if they had lost connection when Kirsten said, "I can't bring myself to question my parents."

"I'm not going to ask my dad straight out either. We need everyone's DNA for cross matching."

"How are we going to manage that without them knowing?"

"Be creative! And let's do it as soon as possible. I'm invited to a barbecue at Dad's house on Sunday and will have to think of something in a hurry. Try to get a sample from each of your parents, and then we'll meet and send everything out together."

Before ending the call, they reassured one another that no matter what the outcome, both were happy to know they were sisters.

****

Moments later, Kirsten called her parents' landline. Might as well get the ball rolling, she decided.

Her mom answered the phone and Kirsten said, "I promised Dad a visit soon. How does this Sunday work for you? It's short notice, but if not this weekend, I won't be able to get away for a long time."

"Sure. We're looking forward to seeing you all," Louise replied.

"It will just be the kids and me, Mike has to work. I'm planning to get to your house between 11:30 and noon and will have to leave by 2:30 at the latest, since we have to be back in San Diego for Ella's dance recital in the evening. I can pick up some lunch, if you like."

"Don't be silly. I'll fix it."

For the rest of the day, while showing a client around a house and later chauffeuring the kids, Kirsten's brain was working overtime, trying to come up with a solution.

Be creative with getting a sample from each parent, her newfound sister had said. A task that seemed difficult to accomplish, Kirsten now considered. She had plenty of ideas but rejected most. There was no way she could make her parents take their own saliva swab or spit into something without rousing their suspicion. Ripping hair samples from their heads was out of the question, and getting them from a hair brush would be tricky at best. She didn't even know if her dad used one.

It wasn't until she lay awake at night, unable to sleep, that she remembered a conversation about toothbrushes that had come up a while back. They had talked about the pros and cons of electric toothbrushes, when Mom had stated that she and Dad preferred to brush the old-fashioned way. She had even mentioned the brand and that she always bought a pink brush for herself and a different color for Dad, in order not to confuse them.

So Kirsten had a brainstorm. It involved running an errand to the drug store on the next day but was otherwise rather simple. With the plan all worked out in her head, she fell asleep in an instant.

Sherry, for her part, was also trying to come up with a useful idea for how to get her dad's DNA. She was considering things like, "Oh no, Dad! A bug flew into your mouth. Spit it out into my tissue," to accidentally pricking him with a sewing needle to catch a drop of blood. That kind of trickery would only work in a novel or movie. She had to do better.

By Saturday morning, she was still without a plan and was getting frantic. She had better come up with a workable solution in a hurry.

Dave found her in the den, cleaning out furniture drawers and shelves.

He said, "Aha! What's the trouble?"

"I don't know what you mean."

"Sure you do. You get into a rush of spring cleaning whenever something's bothering you."

She didn't answer him but came to a sudden halt in her tidiness fit, staring at the object she held in her hand.

"Yes," she murmured to herself, "this will do," and hoped that she could pull it off.

"What did you say?" Dave asked.

"Never mind," she replied, and put everything else back on the shelf.

CHAPTER 25

The ex-hitman had started surveillance right away, and by Saturday he was on the fourth day of shadowing his target. On day one, right off the bat, he had realized that doing the job inside the retirement community was out of the question. The place had tight security.

When he had stepped inside at the front entrance, the receptionist intercepted him and said, "How may I help you, sir?"

"I'd like to have a look around. My aunt is considering moving into a retirement home and I'm doing the legwork for her."

"How nice of you, but we only give tours by appointment. Every so often we have an open house, but you missed the one we had a few days ago. Have a seat. We can give you brochures with information your aunt may find helpful."

And instead of going off to do the errand herself, she reached for the phone on her desk and said, "Carlos, please get me an introduction package when you get a chance."

That had left him no choice but to sit down on one of the upholstered chairs in the lobby instead of staking out the place as planned. He had done one thing right, though, by choosing to show up minutes before noon. Carlos took his time to appear, which worked out fine since a slew of people passed by on their way to the dining hall for lunch.

By pure luck, he overheard one old woman say to another, "Gloria, I want to hear all about your cruise. Is your cold getting better, by the way?"

As they walked by him, he snapped a picture with his smartphone, pretending to be interested in the décor, when in fact he aimed it at the woman he took to be Gloria Morris. In case someone was watching, he got up and took another photo of the entrance to the dining hall. When Carlos came over and handed him several pamphlets of information about the place, it was obvious the man was a security guard. While he wore no uniform, his gait and stance gave him away.

The would-be assassin thanked him and leafed through a price list and info about accommodations and meals, pretending to be interested. There was no longer any reason for him to linger, so he nodded to the receptionist and left the establishment.

He sent the snapshot to the person who had hired him with the words, "Is that her?" The answer in return was, "Yes. She has aged, but there is no mistake."

Tailing the old woman was easy. There was a definite pattern. She walked her small poodle every morning between 9:00 and 9:30, going down the same couple of blocks at a slow pace, seeming to have either leg or hip problems. Then she crossed the street at the end of the block's intersection and walked back to the retirement home on the opposite side of the road. Her routine never changed; she followed the exact same route every day. Whether this was keeping with her own comfort zone or that of her dog's, the ex-mobster did not bother to figure out.

He scouted the area one more time and had his plan down pat. The hit was on for Monday, he decided.

CHAPTER 26

Before Mike left for his 48-hour shift on Saturday, August 15, he asked Kirsten, "What prompted you, out of the blue, to go see your folks tomorrow?"

"No special reason other than a visit to Irvine is overdue and Alex doesn't have any soccer games this weekend. Waiting until everyone in the family is available would take months. I'm sure you don't mind having to miss going."

He grinned and said, "I'm delighted."

The 85-mile drive from San Diego to Irvine on the I-5 took approximately one-and-a-half hours. They left their house at 10:00 in the morning. Before they got onto the freeway, Kirsten glanced at her kids in the rear-view mirror. Ella was reading a book and Alex's fingers were tapping his tablet in rapid, jerky movements.

Observing the road ahead again, she said to her daughter, "You had motion sickness the last time you read while riding, remember?"

"Let me just finish the chapter."

"And you, Alex, leave that thing in the car when we get there. Playing video games while at grandma and grandpa's house would be rude."

With that settled, she turned on the radio and, while listening to music, let her mind go over the task awaiting her in Irvine.

They arrived a few minutes past 11:30, and before getting out of the car Ella asked, "How long are we going to stay?"

"Three hours or so."

"Will I have enough time to get ready for my dance recital?"

"Don't worry, we'll be home in plenty of time."

They rang the doorbell and immediately heard barking coming from within. And when Judge Ericson opened the door, Ember, the salt-and-pepper-colored Schnauzer, ran past him and jumped at Kirsten and the kids in excited greeting. The Judge hugged his daughter and grandkids and they went inside, with Ember wagging her tail and leading the way.

Kirsten found her mom in the kitchen. Smelling the aroma coming from the oven, she said, "You shouldn't have gone through any trouble. Sandwiches would've done."

"No trouble," Mom replied, "I'm fixing quiches. They're almost done and then need to cool for a bit. Go out on the patio. I'll be there in a minute."

Her daughter knew better than to offer her help. The long established fact was that in the Ericson home, the kitchen was Louise's domain, and hers alone.

On the drive over, Kirsten had decided to play the timing of her task by ear. And now, right at the beginning of her visit, she had a perfect opportunity. Mom was in the kitchen, Dad and Alex were playing catch with Ember on the backyard lawn, and she had just seen Ella vanish into the downstairs bathroom. Clutching her purse, she ran up the stairs, taking two steps at the time.

She came to a halt in the master bathroom. To her relief, her parents' toothbrushes were the kind she had expected to find: one pink and one green, and the brand that Mom had said. She took two pre-labeled plastic baggies out of her purse, dropped the corresponding toothbrush in each, zipped them closed, and placed them into her purse. Then she rummaged through her bag and brought out an assortment of new toothbrushes. Besides the pink one, she had bought all of the other colors available; blue, gray, purple, green, and red. She now replaced the green and the pink ones into the toothbrush holder and tossed the others back into her purse.

All this had taken but a few seconds. There was a good chance that neither of her parents would realize their toothbrushes had been exchanged with new ones, and if they did, each would most likely assume that the other had done so. For good measure, she then used the toilet. If someone heard the flushing and then caught her coming down the stairs, it would be obvious that she had been in a hurry while the downstairs bathroom was in use.

The table out on the patio was already set and Louise served them a mixed green salad to start with and then brought out ham, spinach, and cheese quiches. Something for everyone's taste, no doubt. And there was ice cream for dessert. The rest of the afternoon was enjoyed by all, even though Kirsten was plagued with the knowledge that she was there under false pretenses. She also made sure to leave her purse where she could keep an eye on it.

The adults talked about the real estate market, the kids' progress with school and other activities, and Mike's demanding job as a firefighter. The subject of Kirsten's Doppelgänger, however, was avoided. The youngsters never tired of playing with Ember, who reveled in the extra attention. Soon it was 2:30 and time to leave.

CHAPTER 27

At around the same time, the barbecue at Max Andino's house was getting under way. Ben and his family were already there when Sherry and Dave arrived.

Max, clad in an apron with the slogan *Eat at your own risk,* welcomed them and said, "Make yourselves at home. The food should be ready in about 45 minutes." And he stepped into the kitchen, fetched the tri-tip steaks, and carried them out the back door.

The newcomers followed him to the backyard, where they greeted the rest of their clan, while Max headed to the barbecue, which was already fired up. He combined garlic salt and pepper, and then rubbed it over the meat. Ben's daughter stepped closer to her grandpa, who adjusted the rack so it was about three inches from the coals.

She asked, "Why so close?"

As he added the tri-tips to the rack, he explained, "I need to sear the meat over hot coals for about six minutes per side first. Then I'll adjust the rack so the meat is farther from the coals while it continues to cook for another twenty to thirty minutes."

"Who wants to play bocce ball?" Ben asked, walking over to the lawn where the set was placed at the ready.

He found an eager taker in his son, and the daughter, losing interest in watching her grandpa at work, also made her way over to the grassy strip. Dave joined in on the game too. Sherry and Ben's wife passed, stating they would see what help Vanessa needed in the kitchen.

When the meat was ready, the ladies carried hot garlic bread and platters with raw celery, cauliflower, carrots, and cherry tomatoes out from the kitchen. There was a stack of plates, silverware, glasses, and paper napkins placed at the head of the patio table, so everyone served themselves.

Max opened a bottle each of red and white wine. He pointed out, "We have beer and bottled water in the cooler, and help yourselves from the pitcher of lemonade."

At first, all focused on eating the yummy meal, but in due course conversations started to flow. The talk revolved around the colleges Ben's daughter was scouting out and how she was still undecided what to major in.

Then Sherry turned to her nephew and said, "I understand you're good at playing the trumpet. Did you bring it so we can enjoy listening to your music?"

He shook his head, then said with a grin, "I wish *you* were my neighbor."

It was clear that Sherry did not get his meaning, and Ben elaborated, "We have a neighbor who complains about the noise when he practices."

"How rude!" she said with a chuckle.

The conversation turned to Ben's family's upcoming camping trip to Moab, Monument Valley, and the Grand Canyon, and to the new motorhome they had purchased recently.

His wife said, "We're leaving early tomorrow morning and still have some last minute packing to do when we get home."

Addressing Sherry, Vanessa asked, "What are your plans for the rest of the summer?"

"Since we've already taken two trips this year, we're staying put now. Dave is busy at work, and I'm doing a bit of tutoring. Other than that, I plan to just relax until school starts." And she asked, "What about you and Dad? Are you planning a vacation?"

"I'm taking some time off in the fall when resorts are less crowded. We haven't decided where to go yet, though."

Ben inquired of his dad, "How is retirement treating you?"

"Okay, but it gets boring," Max replied.

Vanessa commented, "Your father gives free financial advice. People flock to him for all sorts of freebies and favors. I keep telling him that he should charge them, but he's too goodhearted."

They were done eating when Sherry addressed Dad with, "Oh, I almost forgot." She rummaged in her purse and brought out a small case, asking, "Remember this?"

"My harmonica! Where did you dig that up?"

"Found it yesterday when cleaning out my shelves. You used to play it when we were kids. Think you still can?"

He took it out of its case and said, "Playing an instrument is like riding a bike, one never forgets." He placed it on his lips and started to play a tune. He was a little rusty at first but soon caught on and then went into another melody. Everyone clapped when he stopped playing.

After he put the harmonica back in its case, Sherry grabbed it and placed it in her purse, saying, "I hope you don't mind if I keep it. I cherish the good memories it brings back every time I look at it."

Her dad laughed and said, "I never missed the thing for years so won't miss it now."

****

On their drive home Dave said, "What was all that stuff about having a sentimental tie to that harmonica? You may have fooled your dad but you're not fooling me. Until yesterday, I doubt that you even remembered the mouth organ being in our house. So what's going on?"

Sherry had no choice but to tell him the truth.

He was silent for a long time and finally said, "My advice is to drop your plan right now, while you still can. So you know that you have a sister. Be content with that. It makes sense that the two of you want to start a relationship and meet now and then - - San Diego isn't that far away - - but that should be the extent of it. This plan to get your father's and Kirsten's parents DNA behind their backs is a bad idea. It can only end up in regret for one of you, or both."

"Don't you see? We need to know who's related to who to get any peace of mind. Coming straight out and demanding that they send in their own DNA would be useless. They'd never agree to do it."

There was a stubborn silence between them for the rest of the way home.

Dave was already backing the car down their driveway when he said, "Mark my word. Nothing good will come of this. You'll be sorry you started this whole thing."

CHAPTER 28

The sisters needed to get together pronto. Sherry had the entire day free on Tuesday, August 18, and Kirsten had no appointments to show real estate on that day. And although Mike was on his 48-hours-off schedule, he was planning to go fishing with one of his firefighter buddies. The only obligation Kirsten had was to pick up her kids from school in the late afternoon.

It made sense that Sherry was the one driving from Pasadena to San Diego and not the other way around. The 130-mile journey took approximately two and a quarter hours, so she left her house at 8:30 in the morning, expecting to get there before 11:00. Traffic was heavy starting with the I-210 East freeway, through the CA-57, and the connecting CA-22. It got even worse once she merged onto the I-5 South. It was obvious that she was caught in people's morning commute.

It wasn't until she got out of Orange County that she allowed her mind to wander. She was excited to come face to face again with Kirsten, now that she knew for certain they were sisters. Surely, Kirsten must feel the same way.

Her enthusiasm got a bit clouded as she mulled over what Dave had predicted. His usual lighthearted nature had turned serious when warning her. Could this venture indeed end up in disaster? With each mile closer to her destination she started to have doubts. What if the ultimate DNA results were sad news for her? Would she be able to stomach it?

As Sherry reached the outskirts of San Diego, she told herself, no matter the outcome, I need to know the truth.

Minutes later, guided by the GPS, she parked in front of her sister's home. Kirsten came out to embrace her in a heartfelt hug. Then they took stock of one another.

Kirsten said, "Amazing how much we look alike! Come, I'll give you a quick tour of our house," and she led Sherry through the single-level home consisting of three bedrooms, two baths, living room, dining room, kitchen, and den. The open concept floor plan, open beam ceiling, and hardwood floors throughout gave the place an airy, uncomplicated feel. The roomy, modern, state-of-the-art kitchen looked appealing and practical.

They ended up in the den where Kirsten said, "I have a confession to make. I had second thoughts and almost called you early in the morning to cancel. My conscience is bothering me about doing this in such a sneaky way. And, to be frank, I'm a bit scared about the outcome."

Sherry nodded and admitted, "I had similar thoughts while driving here. Believe me, I hate myself for getting my dad's DNA by tricking him. I'm also upset that we are about to send it and your folks' DNA to be tested without their consent. But, there is no other way, and we have a right to find out the truth."

"Let's go ahead, then!"

So the women gathered the DNA samples of their parents, labeling the plastic baggies containing the toothbrushes and harmonica with the corresponding names. They re-took their own mouth swabs for cross matching, also adding a label on each. Sherry placed all the samples plus paperwork in a large padded envelope and addressed it to Peckingline. Then they drove to the nearest post office together and mailed it.

"Doing this errand jointly feels almost like a ceremony," Sherry commented.

When exiting the building, Kirsten sighed with relief and said, "It's done! No more turning back. Come, Sister, I'll treat you to lunch. I know the perfect place."

"Yes, let's celebrate!"

CHAPTER 29

At 10 o'clock sharp on Thursday morning, August 20, Sherry stepped through the entrance of the main building at the retirement community.

"May I help you?" the receptionist asked.

"Yes, please. I have an appointment to see Gloria Morris. She told me that I'd have to sign in and get directions to her apartment."

The receptionist seemed a bit flustered and said, "Have a seat in the foyer. Robert Wiegert, our executive director, will be with you shortly."

Sherry thought that was odd. Why would the director of the place want to talk with her? As far as she knew, Gloria Morris lived in the independent part of the community and could come and go as she pleased. There was no reason why a visitor would have to be approved. She was about to protest, but the young woman behind the desk was already on the phone with the person in charge.

A bit miffed, Sherry sat down on a comfortable upholstered chair in the reception area. Another person was already there, reading a book. Sherry mused, is he waiting for someone, or expecting to have clearance? The more she thought about being detained instead of directed to the appropriate apartment, the more uneasy she got.

She mulled over the phone conversation she'd had with Gloria. The old lady had been a bit hard of hearing and made her repeat a sentence or two, but she was sharp, there was no doubt about that. She had known right away whom she was talking to, and said that she was looking forward to seeing little Sherry Andino all grown up. She'd mentioned that one needed to sign in at the desk when visiting, but certainly not that a talk with the executive director was customary.

Sherry checked her watch. It was 10:06 already. Gloria may well be annoyed with her for not being on time. The lady belonged to a generation where punctuality was expected as much as truthfulness and cleanliness.

A man in his fifties came over to her with hurried strides and said, "I'm Robert Wiegert, and what is your name?" She gave it.

"I understand that you asked to see Gloria Morris. Are you a relative of hers?"

"No."

"May I ask why you're here?"

There was no mistaking her annoyance as she snapped, "I had an appointment to see the woman at 10:00 a.m. today and am already late."

He said, "I'm sorry but seeing Gloria Morris is impossible. She has moved on."

Taken aback, Sherry said, "She didn't mention anything about moving. Do you have her new address?"

"You misunderstand. She has passed away."

Sherry was speechless for a few seconds and then said, "She told me about getting over a cold but I had no idea that she was seriously ill."

"She was not sick. On Monday of this week, dear Gloria was killed by a hit-and-run driver while walking her dog."

"How horrible! Is the driver behind bars?"

"No, the authorities are still looking for him." And Mr. Wiegert asked, "Were you and Gloria close?"

"Not really. She knew me when I was a small child and agreed to give me some information about my family for the memoir I'm writing." She surprised herself as she realized how easily that lie had come out of her mouth.

"I see. Well, I'm sorry to have had to inform you of the sad news." He turned and left her in a rush to get away, taking big strides in the direction of the hallway.

Sherry had gotten to her feet when Robert Wiegert appeared but sat back down now. She needed to process what she had just learned. Hit-and-run accidents happened way too often these days, she pondered. Even though she had not known her, she felt sorry for the old lady who had met with such a violent death.

The receptionist stood next to her, all of a sudden, and said, "It's so sad about Gloria. She was one of my favorite people. So full of life. It was not time yet for her to go."

Sherry asked, "Do you know any details about the accident?"

"There were a couple of witnesses. One is a tenant of our community who told me what she saw. Gloria took

Princess, her poodle, for a walk on Monday, like she did every day. She was a bit hard of hearing and unaware of the speeding car coming at her when she was in the crosswalk at the end of the block. By the time she was aware of the speeding idiot, it was too late. Gloria was knocked unconscious and, as far as I heard, stayed comatose until she died of internal bleeding. She must have let go of the leash, though, because Princess was able to escape."

"Was the witness you talked to able to recognize the make of the car and get a glimpse of the driver?"

"A dark color SUV with tinted windows is all she could remember seeing, and there was no license plate on the car. The person came at great speed, ran her down, and then raced away, not even slowing down after the hit."

Sherry thanked her for the information and got up to leave.

CHAPTER 30

There was another rendezvous in the park. The hitman approached the bench occupied by the person he had met earlier and sat down a foot away from the individual's bag.

Avoiding eye contact he said, "The job is done. Fatal hit-and-run."

"I know; it was mentioned in the news," the other person stated. "I hope you took precautions not to get caught."

Insulted, the former said, "I'm not a moron. The hit-car was dark gray with no license plates. Mine is bright red, without any dents and with legit plates, front and back. I repaired the damage to the bumper and did the new paint job myself. It helps to be a Jack-of-all-trades.

"As for the scene, I made sure that there were few witnesses. I saw an old woman ambling along the sidewalk, but I'm sure she couldn't give the cops any useful info. There was one car driving a distance behind me before impact. I noticed in the rearview mirror that he stopped at the scene, and I made sure no vehicles chased after me."

"Spare me the details," the other said.

"As you wish."

"Don't tell anyone that we've seen each other recently, not even Junior."

"You think I'm some kind of an amateur? Just because I've become legit doesn't mean I've lost the touch."

"Sure. I didn't mean to insult you. The balance payment is all here. I counted it twice."

Nothing more was said. The person who had arrived first got up and left, leaving the bag behind. The other stayed put until the former was out of sight and then seized the sack in a relaxed manner and strolled off in the opposite direction.

CHAPTER 31

Gloria Morris had made funeral arrangements for her own demise years earlier in order to take that burden off her son. Every aspect was pre-planned and paid for: the cremation, funeral memorial ceremony, type of container for the ashes, and the exact spot of her final resting place. Each detail was carefully documented, including the memorial tablet marking the location where her ashes would be interred.

There was a fair group of mourners gathered for the memorial ceremony at one of Forest Lawn's chapels on Tuesday morning, August 25. Gloria's son, daughter-in-law, and their two young adult kids were the only living relatives of the dead woman. Her siblings had long passed before her. The rest of the assembled were old friends, past co-workers, and newly made friends of her retirement community. Bob Tully and a man in his eighties - - the two survivors of the former bridge club - - were among the mourners.

The ceremony started with Gloria's granddaughter taking the lead, saying, "Here is grandma's favorite tune," proceeding to play it on her flute. There was no designated person giving a formal rehearsed eulogy. Instead, some mourners got up and on the spur of the moment stood in front of the congregation, paying tribute to Gloria by mentioning little anecdotes from her life. Some were amusing, others touching. Bob Tully shared a couple of the witty comments his bridge partner had made after beating their opponents in the game.

At the end of the service, Kurt Morris, Gloria's son, invited everyone to a luncheon reception at the retirement community. People caravanned out of Forest Lawn to the next venue. Once arrived, they were joined by many of the community's residents who had not been able to make the trip to the mortuary. The lunch consisted of chicken with vegetables and mashed potatoes. Chocolate chip cookies were offered for dessert.

At the funeral home, people had been careful to avoid conversations about the manner of Gloria's death, but during the luncheon, at the cozy setting of the community's dining hall, they felt less restrained.

Bob Tully happened to sit next to one of the witnesses of the accident, who had no scruples about telling him what she saw. After going over in detail that she had walked to a drug store two blocks away on that morning before it got too hot, she finally came to the point and stated, "If you ask me, the driver of that SUV ran her down on purpose."

"What makes you think so?" Bob inquired.

"It was broad daylight. There was no way that he could have missed seeing them. Gloria and Princess were in the crosswalk when he came speeding along and plowed into her full force."

"The person driving the SUV was a man?"

"Or it could have been a woman. The car had tinted windows. I just said 'he' for convenience, meaning the driver. And since he didn't slow down afterward, let alone stop, it makes me suspicious that it was done on purpose." And she added, "But who would've wanted to kill Gloria? She didn't seem to have had any enemies. Just the opposite; she was well liked."

"Were there more witnesses?"

"There was another driver, a man who stopped and ran over to where Gloria lay."

She shivered and said, "By the time I made it to the ghastly scene too - - I can't run any longer - - the man was trying to find her pulse, which was weak. Gloria was unconscious, looking horrible, all distorted and bloody. I called 911, and the police and paramedics came real fast. We learned later that she got to the hospital 'dead on arrival,' having sustained internal bleeding."

Bob tried to enjoy his lunch but had lost his appetite. What he had learned from his table-neighbor gave him much to think about.

At one point during the luncheon, Kurt Morris thanked everyone for coming. Then he said, "We have not found a permanent home for Princess, Mom's poodle, yet. My wife is highly allergic to any kind of furry pets, so we cannot have Princess living with us. Right now, she is temporarily staying with a tenant of this community. Let me know if any of you are interested in adopting her. She is four years old, is current with all her shots, and has a good disposition."

As the luncheon reception came to an end, Bob went over to Gloria's family to express his condolences.

Kurt said, "Mom often talked about what a great friend and bridge partner you were to her, starting back at the Acorn Forest Apartments and continuing for decades."

"That goes both ways; I cherish her memory." Bob then said, "About Princess. I'd like to give her a home but need to check with my partner first."

"Oh, sure. Call me if you decide to take her," and he gave him his number.

CHAPTER 32

On that evening after dinner, Bob and Ralph lingered over coffee at their home in South Pasadena. The couple's dialogue went like this:

Ralph said, "I've got everything under control for Saturday's outdoor wedding in Malibu. The cake will be delivered one hour before the reception and we can pick up the table centerpieces from the florist at 12:00 noon. We're getting lots of help with the food catering, but you already know that. And we'll have to - - -"

He stopped in mid-sentence, asking, "Are you listening?"

Bob said, "No, I wasn't. Sorry! You should have come to the funeral. Although you and I didn't have anything to do with planning the event, it turned out nice."

"Somebody had to mind the business! Besides, I wouldn't have come even if I had the time. Not only do I hate funerals, but I didn't know the old lady who died. As to your other remark, we don't do funerals and never will. And how can you call such an occasion 'nice'?"

"No matter what your feelings are about funerals, the memorial ceremony *was* nice. Nobody gave a eulogy but lots of people shared stories about Gloria's life. She was well liked; that was evident."

Ralph said, "I know you liked her and I'm sorry for your loss, but can we change the subject now?"

Bob was not done yet. He said, "Did I tell you that Gloria was walking her poodle when she got killed by the hit-and-run driver?"

"Yes, I remember you saying so."

"The poodle survived. Her name is Princess and she needs a new home. How about if we give her one?"

"Forget it!" Ralph said. "You know that's not going to work with Snicker. He'd scratch the poodle's eyes out. Also, a dog needs lots of attention and we're too busy to take her for walks."

"You're right. I didn't think this through." And before his partner had a chance to steer the talk back to their business, Bob went on, "At the luncheon, I sat next to a woman who witnessed the accident. She's of the opinion that the driver ran Gloria down on purpose."

"The woman most likely made that up to feel important. Don't dwell on it."

"But I do and can't shake the unpleasant thought that Gloria may have been murdered."

"You've been reading too many mystery novels."

Bob went on, "You don't understand. I called Sherry Rinaldi earlier today, asking if she got a chance to meet with Gloria. Guess what? Sherry had an appointment to see her last Thursday!"

"What has that got to do with anything?"

"Don't you see? It can't be a coincidence that Gloria conveniently dies three days before she is scheduled to talk with Sherry."

"You're correct. I don't understand in the least. According to you, the purpose of their meeting was for Gloria to help Sherry with the research for the memoir she's writing. Now you're suggesting that the old woman needed to be silenced. That is extremely farfetched. What shattering secret could she possibly reveal?"

"A murder gone unpunished."

"Now you've lost touch with reality altogether!"

Bob said, "I've given this a lot of thought since the call with Sherry. Her mom drowned in the apartment complex's pool 40 years ago. It went on record as an accidental drowning. I think it's feasible that it wasn't an accident and that someone killed her."

"Be reasonable. If Gloria would have either witnessed or known of such a killing, it makes sense that she'd have notified the authorities at the time."

"It may be more complicated than that."

Ralph wagged a finger at Bob and exclaimed, "You're the one who's making it complicated. Like I said, reading all those books about murder and mayhem is making you unrealistic. This entire thing is a fabrication of your imagination."

"What if it's not? Don't you think Sherry has a right to know the truth about what happened to her mother? And Gloria's son deserves to get the facts behind the hit-and-run accident of his mother too."

"I beg to differ. Even if you were right - - and I'm positive that you're wrong - - what they don't know couldn't hurt them."

Snicker jumped into Ralph's lap at that moment and he said to the cat, "You agree?" Snicker blinked and started to knead his thighs, and then settled down for a nap.

Bob could not let it go and said, "The witness I talked with at the funeral luncheon was certain that the driver ran Gloria down on purpose."

"There you have it! It was because of that woman's word alone that your imagination is running wild. You sat next to her by pure chance. Had the cards dealt you a different table-neighbor, we wouldn't be having this conversation. None of this is any of your concern. Keep your nose out of it."

Bob cried out, "The diary!"

"What are you talking about now?"

"I just remembered that Gloria kept one. She even made a joke about me being able to read people's old sins in it once she passed on. I bet she noted all her observations in that journal, including what she knew or suspected about the drowning of Sherry's mother."

Ralph got up, and as he cleared the coffee cups away said, "Now you're making things up again! Snap out of your fantasy land already and get back to the real world. We've got some business decisions to make."

For the rest of the evening there was only shop talk on their agenda.

CHAPTER 33

Sherry and Kirsten were informed of the DNA results simultaneously on Thursday, August 27. Each received a cover letter from Peckingline stating that their samples contained enough DNA to make a precise analysis and that their DNA cross-match findings were 90% accurate. The enclosed document held the following data:

Kirsten Hiller and Louise Ericson = a match

Kirsten Hiller and Judge Ericson = a match

Kirsten Hiller and Max Andino = no match

Sherry Rinaldi and Louise Ericson = no match

Sherry Rinaldi and Judge Ericson = a match

Sherry Rinaldi and Max Andino = no match

Kirsten stared at the results for a long time before the full meaning registered. So as far as she was concerned, the findings verified the status quo of being her parents' only child. The bombshell exposed was that Dad had fathered Sherry. And the thought hit her; what ghastly news this must be for Sherry. Her first impulse was to reach for the phone to console her half-sister, but she changed her mind and decided to give her time to digest the knowledge.

****

Dave closed the door to his office in Studio City, leaving behind another stressful day. While driving home, he tried to close his mind to all work-related matters and concentrated on what lay ahead. He was looking forward to a nice supper with his wife, then watching a movie on Netflix, and maybe getting friendly later on. All this was not going to happen.

Dave found Sherry in the kitchen. She was standing on a stepping-stool, cleaning out the top shelf of the walk-in pantry. He thought, she's into spring cleaning again. This can't be good.

Aloud he said, "What's for dinner, Honey?"

"I'm not hungry!"

The evidence of her distress was left on the kitchen table. Dave read the printout of Peckingline's findings twice to make sure he understood its meaning. When Sherry stepped off the stool to face him, her red, swollen eyes told the whole story.

He did not say "I told you so" but drew her close in a hug, where she promptly started to weep again.

Releasing her, he said, "It's not the end of the world."

"How would you like to discover that the man who raised you with tender love is in fact not your father?" she shot back between sobs.

"There's the key word. He brought you up with love, and his affection for you holds to date."

She shrugged.

Dave said, "When you sent in those DNA samples for cross-matching, you must have had an inkling of this outcome."

"Maybe, but I didn't want to believe it." And after a pause she added, "What hurts the most is his deception."

"It's possible that he doesn't know that you're not his child."

Sherry thought about it for some time and then said, "When I first questioned him about the swapping that went on in the Acorn Forest Apartments, he said that there had been strict rules about birth control protection."

"So that proves my point that he may not have known."

She shook her head and said, "Maybe not then. But now that I've made him aware of having met a lookalike woman who lived in those apartments at the same time, he should at least have doubts."

Dave said, "Has it occurred to you that the news would be as painful for him as it is for you?"

She admitted, "I hadn't thought about that. I was just mad at him all day. In time, when I've come to better terms with it myself, I'll show him Peckingline's document."

"I wouldn't do that."

"Why not? He deserves to know the truth."

"Don't tell him, is my advice. You have a good relationship with Max. There is nothing to be gained by exposing the truth to him, which would only cause him suffering. Continue to call him 'Dad' and treat him as such."

"Easy for you to say," she shot back.

He squeezed her hand and remarked, "Now return all that stuff to the walk-in pantry and I'll call in a pizza delivery order."

CHAPTER 34

On Friday, Kirsten mulled over the phone call she had just ended with Sherry. As expected, the DNA results had hit her half-sister hard. She tried to put herself in Sherry's place. How would she herself react if faced with the knowledge that her own dad was not the man who fathered her? Unthinkable! It was hard enough to deal with the knowledge of her own parents' transgressions and her dad fathering Sherry.

Sherry had mentioned that she was not planning to tell her dad - - meaning Max Andino - - about their discovery. At least not for the moment. Likewise, Kirsten had no intention of letting her parents know. She could picture her dad being embarrassed and ashamed when confronted with the news, and there was no way of knowing how her mom would respond. She might play deaf and block it from her mind, or go into a rage. Maybe it was best to keep them all in the dark.

A sudden memory of a dialogue she had had with her mom popped into her mind. At about twelve or thirteen she had asked, "Was it you or Dad, or both of you, who only wanted to have one child?"

"Oh, darling," Mom had replied, "You've got that all wrong. We would have wanted nothing more than be able to give you siblings. Unfortunately, there were complications at your birth which made it impossible for me to get pregnant again."

Kirsten remembered seeing tears in her mom's eyes when she made that statement. She now reflected that given Mom's condition, even over four decades later, the discovery that Dad had fathered another child with someone else could throw her into an even deeper depression.

Her mind was made up; she would spare her parents the agony of learning the truth. But should she tell Mike? As a rule she kept no secrets from her husband, but in this case she was undecided. And under no circumstances did she want the kids to know. How could she explain their grandparents' escapades into wife/husband swapping?

Another thought occurred to her. She had already formed a relationship with Sherry and had no regrets about it. The two had clicked immediately and there was no denying their existing bond. But could they keep their connection a secret from their folks in the long run? Even if they pretended to be only friends, their striking resemblance would belie their words.

Her phone vibrated with a text from Alex:

"Where are you, Mom?"

Kirsten checked the time. Rats! she thought, I should have picked him up from soccer practice 15 minutes ago.

She texted back, *"Sorry! I'm on my way."* and flew out the door.

CHAPTER 35

To Bob Tully's surprise, he received a call from Kurt Morris on Tuesday morning, September 1.

Before Gloria's son could give him any news, Bob said, "Sorry my partner and I couldn't take Princess. Did you find her a new owner?"

"Yes. The person from the retirement community who took care of her temporarily fell in love with her and decided to give her a permanent home. But that's not why I'm calling. Mom made a will and was specific about some of her possessions. She left you her luxury chess set."

"Are you serious? I'm inheriting her Staunton ebony chess set?"

"Yes, sir."

"How generous of her! I'm thrilled to pieces. I always admired the fine craftsmanship of the ebony and Kari wood chessmen. The hand-crafted ebony board alone is exquisite. I feel honored that Gloria wanted me to have the set, and I'll take good care of it." Bob was glad the other could not see the tears of gratitude welling up in his eyes.

Kurt said, "You live in South Pasadena, which is close by Arcadia where we are. Do you mind coming by some day and picking the set up? I'd rather not ship it to avoid taking the risk of damaging it."

"Not at all," Bob replied, and they picked a date and time. And he asked, "Have you read your mom's diary?"

"What diary?"

"She kept one."

"That's news to me. My wife and I went through her belongings. We put some things in storage until we decide what to do with them, and gave others to the Goodwill. As far as I know, we did not come across any diary. Why do you ask?"

Bob said, "Last time I came to visit Gloria at her retirement community, she said I could read things that happened in the Acorn Forest Apartments when we both lived there in her diary, once she was gone."

"That's a weird thing to say."

"I know. So you can see why I'm curious."

Kurt promised to ask his wife whether she had seen the journal, and they ended the call.

The following morning Kurt called back with the news that his wife thought the diary may have gone to the Goodwill among several boxes of books. He mentioned that they did not have room in their home to keep so many books and had taken them from his mom's living room shelves and boxed them up to get rid of, without taking the time to look at each one.

When asked if he wouldn't mind if Bob tried to retrieve the journal from the Goodwill place, Kurt said, "By all means, go ahead," and gave him the address.

CHAPTER 36

Getting a hold of Gloria's diary was not an easy task as Bob soon found out. He knew that driving to the Goodwill store without delay was essential, before someone else showed an interest in that journal. He opted to have a late breakfast with the idea of skipping lunch and was on his way. Ralph was out, giving a potential new client an estimate. So Bob sent him a quick text with the message, "Running an errand of my own. See you soon."

The Goodwill store was in Pasadena, so he got there in record time. The manager was a middle-aged woman who was eager to help.

Bob said, "A diary was included by accident with a recent donation of books from Kurt Morris. I hope to buy it back if it's still here."

She said, "I remember. That was last Saturday. We kept what we have room for on our shelves and sent the rest to one of our other stores." She led him to the appropriate bookshelf, saying, "Feel free to take your time to go through the books," and left him to it.

He was looking at about 200 or so books. They had not been ordered according to category, edition, or size, but stood jumbled on the shelf. Most hardcover copies were missing their jackets, and some of the paperbacks had seen better days. There was a sign stating, "Hardcovers $3.00; paperbacks $2.00." Bob inspected each work with care. He came across a mystery novel by Dick Francis he could not resist, but Gloria's diary was not among the bunch. He had already spent an hour in the place and now checked out the rest of the store in case the journal had been placed in a different section.

Again unsuccessful, he went in search of the manager and found her in an alcove, putting price tags on merchandise that had come in. She asked, "No luck?"

"I'm afraid not," he replied. "You mentioned that part of Kurt Morris's donation went to a different location. Where is that?"

"Our driver delivered it to the store in San Remo yesterday with other merchandise we have no room for here." And she gave him the address.

He went over to the young woman behind the cash register and paid for the Dick Francis book, then drove to San Remo.

The Goodwill store in San Remo was larger than the one Bob had visited in Pasadena. He had to consult several employees until he found one who could give him information pertaining to his quest.

The young man in charge said, "Yes, we received a bunch of stuff from Pasadena yesterday, among them some boxes of books. We haven't gotten around to pricing and putting them out on the shelves yet. Come back in a couple days and all should be out and ready for sale."

Bob said, "The diary in question is not only extremely personal but may hold information that is essential to me. I can't take the risk of it being picked up by someone else. May I have a brief look into the boxes of books?"

The man seemed undecided for a moment and then said, "In general, we don't bring customers to the back room, but I can see that this is important to you. Follow me." And he led the way to a storage room off the main store. He pointed to four open boxes sitting on the floor and said, "These are all the books that came in yesterday. Have a look but don't take too long. I need to get back up front soon."

There were about 20 to 25 books in each box that Bob rummaged through, by taking them out one at a time and then replacing them back into the box. The young man stood close by and extended a helping hand. Two thirds into the last box and ready to throw in the towel, he saw it! Instead of a jacket, cardboard or paper cover, the thick book of several 100 pages had a velvety fabric cover of burgundy color. There was no title or author name.

"This must be the journal!" Bob exclaimed, unable to hide his excitement.

He opened it to the front page, which his friend had filled out in cursive handwriting as follows:

Diary of: *Gloria Morris*

Place of birth: *California, USA*

Date of birth: *June 15, 1936*

Profession: *Accountant*

Interests: *Reading, playing bridge, chess, collecting antiques*

"Yes, this is definitely what I'm looking for," Bob stated.

The store clerk was debating whether to charge $3.00 or $2.00 for the diary when the former said, "It's priceless to me, but I'll give you $10.00 for it."

On his way home he drove by the Acorn Forest Apartments and thought how funny it was that the diary ended up in the town of San Remo, not far from where Gloria had spent a few years of her life. On impulse - - despite hardly being able to wait to read the diary - - he stopped and parked the car, then walked to the entrance of the apartment complex.

The place had not changed much in 40 years. The exterior stucco of the buildings was now painted a different color but structure-wise they looked the same. He walked over to the small playground where two mothers were chatting while watching their toddlers on the swings. He peeked into the adjacent laundry room and noticed the updated washers and dryers were in use, but overall the room looked the way it had when he had lived there.

The manager's office was still in building A at ground level, and he briefly reasoned that the man who had held that position then would be long dead. He went over to the pool area and peered over its fence. There were only a couple of people swimming, and a small child played in the wading pool while his mother kept a watchful eye on him. Nobody occupied the launch chairs. Bob was not surprised to see the area almost deserted on a Tuesday afternoon in September. The kids were back in school and the adults at work.

Building B was on the opposite side of the pool. Bob looked up to its second floor, thinking, there's my apartment. And he dwelled on the many times he had sat out on the balcony, reading or watching people swimming. He shuddered when remembering the commotion by the pool on the night they had found Sherry's mom.

He turned in a hurry and walked out of the complex, wondering what had possessed him to stop by.

CHAPTER 37

"Where have you been all day?" asked Ralph as soon as Bob stepped into the foyer of their home.

"It's a long story, but guess what I found?" Bob replied, holding the journal up in the air like a trophy.

"What's that? A book from the Victorian era?"

"Not even close. It's Gloria's diary and I'm eager to dive into it."

"It will have to wait until after dinner. I need your help preparing it." And while they walked toward the kitchen Ralph continued, "I'm putting an enchilada casserole together and would like you to toss a salad. The lettuce, tomatoes, and celery aren't washed yet. And please chop the onion for me; you know how I can't stop crying when doing it."

While they worked side by side, Bob told of his day's exploration, at the end of which Ralph commented, "I sure hope chasing after that diary was worth your trouble and you won't be disappointed. I can imagine it contains mostly boring stuff from the woman's day-to-day life."

"Gloria was not a boring person," Bob stated.

"And what was the reason you went to those apartments in San Remo?"

"I wish I knew! When driving by, I had a sudden urge to check out the place. I found it little changed, by the way."

With dinner consumed and the dishes cleared away, Bob got comfortable in the study. At long last, he was free to read the diary, which spanned over Gloria's life time, starting with her marriage. It was handwritten, and he was thankful that she had good penmanship that was precise and easy to read.

The first entry read, *"I got this diary as a wedding present and might as well make use of it."* Each entry was dated and at times there were big gaps between postings. It seemed to Bob that she only wrote about events and happenings that she considered important. Some of the entries only stated the facts and others went into specifics and revealed her feelings. For instance, after the birth of her son, she described taking care of her baby in great detail, whereas the end of her marriage was dealt with in two sentences: *"My suspicion was well founded. I caught him cheating, so I divorced the SOB."*

During her residence at the Acorn Forest Apartments in San Remo she had posted often and sometimes at length. Some of the entries pertained to her son as a high school student: his grades, participation in sports, and going to school dances, *et cetera*. She wrote about friends she had made while living in the apartment complex and elaborated on the bridge club. Bob could not help but smile as he read, "*We have formed a bridge club and play every other Wednesday evening, taking turns hosting it. My bridge partner is a delightful young man by the name of Bob Tully. He's a sharp dresser, witty, and an excellent player. He has even beaten me at chess, once or twice.*"

She noted some general happenings involving tenants of the apartments, mostly harmless stuff she seemed to have ferreted out. There was mention of the wife/husband swapping, and from whom she had learned of it. She did not judge, simply stated the fact. There were other bits and pieces of gossip about her fellow residents but since Bob did not remember or may have never known them, he skimmed over it. His senses sharpened, however, when he started to read about an incident she described that took place at the apartments' playground and the adjacent laundry room.

He read on, and all of a sudden yelled out aloud, "Oh, no!"

Ralph, who had been typing an invoice, looked up from his laptop and asked, "What's wrong?"

"Come and look at this!"

Ralph started reading the text in the diary where Bob's finger was pointed and kept reading for the next two pages.

Then he gazed at his partner and stated, "That's quite an accusation she's making!"

"I'll say. It's an allegation of murder."

"She had no proof, though. That's why she kept quiet."

Bob said, "I can't let this rest."

"And your plan is?"

"I don't know yet, but we can't let the culprit go unpunished."

"I don't like the word 'we' you used. Keep me out of it. The case went down as accidental drowning 40 years ago. What makes you think you can persuade anyone of authority to look into it now? If your friend could not find evidence then, how do you propose to find it now?"

"Gloria's murder may be easier to prove. After all, it happened only two weeks ago. And it stands to reason that both crimes are linked."

"Well, good luck! They may never find the hit-and-run driver, let alone prove that the person ran her over on purpose."

"Gloria named the guilty party in her diary. I'll go from there."

"Don't get involved, Bob, I beg you."

"Gloria was a good friend and I want justice for her."

"That doesn't mean you have to stick out your neck and get yourself into danger."

"Don't worry, I'll be careful."

Ralph shrugged and went back to his task of typing the invoice.

Bob continued reading the diary where he had left off. Nothing more was written in it pertaining to her suspicion of murder. It contained the next four decades of Gloria's life. And although interesting, those pages did not help him with his quest.

The very last entry read, "*I am about to meet Sherry Andino, Emma's daughter, again. Her name is Rinaldi now, and I'm curious to see what kind of a woman she has become.*

My recollection of her is of a sweet, blond toddler. According to Bob Tully, the woman is writing her memoir and wants to talk with me about life in the apartment complex we shared so long ago. I have mixed feelings about that. Does she deserve to know the truth about what happened to her mom, or should I spare her the agony? I'll play it by ear."

It was past midnight and Ralph had long gone to bed when Bob read that last entry. He closed the diary and placed it in their safe.

CHAPTER 38

Vanessa, Max Andino's girlfriend, asked him, "What's going on with you? You're on edge lately."

"I don't want to talk about it," he said.

They happened to be on an after-dinner walk through the neighborhood park in Arcadia. Without warning, she pulled him to a sudden halt and blocked his way. She then planted her face two inches from his and said, "Try me! We've been together for three years. Whatever it is that's bothering you affects me too."

Max was stunned by her intensity and as she released him said, "If you have to know, I'm worried about Sherry."

That figures, she thought. It's always about Sherry, who comes first and foremost with him. Aloud she said, "Tell me."

He was reluctant but realized that there was no way around it. Some of his past had to be exposed, and he debated on what and how much.

As they continued their walk he stared straight ahead and said, "Sherry thinks that she has a sister, or at least a half-sister, and she's also doubtful that I may not be her real father."

After a long pause Vanessa asked, "Well, does she and aren't you?"

"I don't know, dammit!"

She mulled this over and then said, "What makes Sherry get an idea like that?"

So he told her about the Doppelgänger Sherry had met on her Hawaiian trip and how one thing led to another where she and her double were concerned. He mentioned that the two women were in contact and that they were aware of having lived in the same apartment complex as little girls.

Vanessa took a deep breath and then said, "Not to speak ill of the dead, but do you believe it's possible that your wife cheated on you?"

"Emma was not to blame, but there is a remote possibility that someone else fathered Sherry." And he had no choice but to tell her about the wife/husband swapping.

Vanessa burst out laughing. "So you dabbled with the swinging crowd! That's hilarious."

"There's nothing funny about it. I've regretted the experience ever since. And I think you're confusing the term 'swinging.' I believe those people were called the swinging singles. The swapping we did was among married couples."

Seconds later he added, "I still don't understand how it could have happened, if indeed it happened. There were strict rules about protection within the group."

They turned around at the edge of the park and were homeward bound when she asked, "Did your wife suspect - - I mean - - did you two discuss the possibility?"

He clammed up and barked, "That's none of your damned business!"

They strode in silence and Vanessa thought, he sure is touchy where his wife is concerned. I don't know what to make of it. And then another thought occurred to her: if in Max's shoes, I'd have DNA tests done to learn the truth. But she knew better than to bring that up.

They had reached the front yard of Max's house when he stated, "I'd do and give anything to keep my good father/daughter relationship with Sherry."

"I bet!" she said under her breath.

CHAPTER 39

With the new school year at its start, Sherry immersed herself wholeheartedly in her teaching profession and dwelled less on the past. To a certain degree she even came to accept it. Likewise, Kirsten was too busy with her job and tending to the needs of her family to stay preoccupied with what had happened 40 years earlier.

The only one who was not about to let it rest was Bob Tully. By the end of the first week of September, he had formed a plan of action. His mind was made up and nobody could make him change it. Still, he opted to run his decision by Ralph.

He waited until they had taken care of business for the day and then said, "I'm going to hire Hawk to look into the killings of Gloria and Sherry's mother."

"Who's Hawk?"

"Don't you remember? He recovered equipment that was stolen from us a few years ago."

"Oh, the private investigator. I never understood why he wouldn't use his real name. I recall that he even printed his business cards with just 'Hawk,' no first and last name. And he was kind of scary looking. Are you sure you want to get involved with him?"

"I'm positive. He's licensed and gets results."

"And doesn't come cheap," Ralph said. "I can't justify using the business's expense account for something like that."

Bob assured him. "I'll pay him out of my own pocket."

"What exactly can you give Hawk as far as leads, information, clues, or whatever you want to call it?"

"In Emma's case there is the diary, which speaks volumes. And the motive also stands to reason. As for Gloria's murder, there is the witness who is convinced that the driver ran her down on purpose. The motive of course is self-preservation. Gloria was the only person who knew about what happened and needed to be silenced."

"All indirect stuff and no real evidence. I believe they call it hearsay in a court of law."

Bob raised his eyes up to the ceiling in frustration and stated, "Don't you see? That's where Hawk comes in. He'll gather the needed evidence so the two cases can go to court. And since they are linked, they may even be prosecuted together in the same trial."

"Are you planning to inform Sherry of what you're up to?"

"In the end, she will have to know, and I believe deserves to know, but for the time being, there's no need to get her involved."

"What about Gloria's son?"

"He, too, doesn't need to know just yet."

Ralph had the last word by saying, "I think you're in over your head and hope it won't backfire on you. And for God's sake, be careful! Keep in mind what happened to your friend Gloria."

CHAPTER 40

Instead of Hawk's office, the initial consultation meeting was held at Bob and Ralph's house the day after Labor Day, on Tuesday, September 8. Bob was not even sure that the private investigator had an office.

As a rule, guests were asked to take off their shoes in the foyer before entering the home's interior. There were different sizes of slippers available next to the shoe rack. However, Bob lacked the courage to demand this of Hawk. The man had a shaved head and a scar that started at his left eyebrow and stretched halfway down that side of his cheek, and he towered over Bob by eight inches. Regardless of the 90-degree heat outside, he was dressed in jeans, a sport coat, and cowboy boots. And no doubt, he was packing heat.

As he ushered him into the study Bob said, "I don't know if you remember me."

Hawk replied, "Sure do. Never forget a face. I remember this house too."

"May I offer you something to drink?"

"I'm good."

They sat down and Hawk asked, "Isn't your partner around?"

"No. This is a private matter and has nothing to do with our business or Ralph. I would like to hire you to investigate what I suspect are two murders, one recent, the other committed 40 years ago. They both are recorded as accidents."

"I see. Let's talk money first."

"I believe your hourly rate was $60.00 when we hired you last time?"

"That was a few years back. I now charge $80.00 an hour plus mileage and other expenses. Today's consultation is free, whether or not I take the case."

Bob thought that was steep but felt he had no choice and said, "I can do that."

"Sure you can, considering your posh house in this upscale neighborhood of South Pasadena." And he looked him in the eye and said, "Let's cut to the chase. Tell me all about those accidents that you suspect are killings, and I'll decide whether or not I'll take on the job."

So Bob did just that, explaining step by step what he had learned. At the end of his monologue, he went over to the fireplace and took Gloria's diary from the mantel.

He opened it to the appropriate entry and said, "See for yourself."

Hawk took his time reading the applicable pages of text. When he at last looked up, he commented, "Interesting! What is your connection to these people?"

"Nothing other than that I lived in the same apartment complex at the time they did. I hardly knew them, but Gloria Morris was my friend and I want justice for her."

Hawk stared straight ahead and was silent for what felt to Bob like an eternity. He jumped when the private eye all of a sudden stated, "I'm taking the case; it interests me."

He removed a small notebook and pen from the inside pocket of his coat jacket, consulted the journal again, and wrote down the person's name whom Gloria had accused and made some other notes as well. Next he asked Bob for information about the witness to Gloria's hit-and-run accident. Bob was prepared and handed him a piece of paper with the woman's name and the address of the retirement community she resided in.

Hawk said, "I need to ask you again, do you know the person accused in this journal?"

"As I said, we lived in the same apartment complex I told you about, but that was 40 years ago. I didn't know the individual well then and had no contact after we both moved away."

Pointing at the diary Hawk said, "Taken from the piece of information in there, I have a name to start with, so the person shouldn't be hard to track down. If the individual still lives in Southern California and can be linked to the hit-and-run, we're in luck. If not, the case is more complicated and will take time."

Then he said, "I'll need a retainer of $350."

Bob went over to the bureau to get his personal checkbook, wrote out the check, and as he handed it over, Hawk said, "I'll get in touch with you when I have something to report, at which point the first invoice becomes due."

Without another word, he pulled his lanky frame out of the chair and left.

CHAPTER 41

On the following Monday, Hawk made his next appearance. He preferred to conduct business in person, never by e-mail, phone, or text message. A quick call was necessary to schedule appointments, but nothing was ever discussed by phone. "Less messy that way," he claimed.

When settled in the study, he started his report by saying, "Our suspect was easy to locate. As far as connecting the person to the hit-and-run, that's a negative. I talked to the woman who witnessed Gloria Morris's accident and she is credible in my opinion. She described the scene and also the vehicle involved. I cannot link the car to our suspect, who doesn't own such an SUV. Also, I checked all car rentals in every county of Southern California; from L. A. and Orange County, all the way to San Bernardino and Ventura. Nobody returned such a vehicle with a damaged front. Needless to say that the police have not identified the driver and I'm sure they never will."

Disappointed, Bob opened his mouth but Hawk held up his hand before he could speak and said, "I'm not finished. I told you during our consultation that it may be more complicated. Not only can't the car be linked to the accused mentioned in your friend's diary, but the person also has a foolproof alibi for the time the hit-and-run occurred on Monday, August 17. Our suspect may have hired an assassin."

"Oh, my God!"

"As you can imagine, people don't pick up the yellow pages or consult the internet to find one. I'll have to do some research to determine if the suspect has - - or had in the past - - any connection to the mob."

Bob's eyes got as big as saucers as he asked, "You mean the Italian mafia?"

"Maybe, but there exist all sorts of mafias, besides the Italian. If there is such a connection, I'll go from there. In the meantime, I have a request."

"Sure."

"It's about the daughter of the drowning victim. I take it that she's unaware of possibly having a half-sister. Get in touch and inform her of the claim Gloria made. In order to prove or disprove it, we'll need DNA from both women. Get her consent and then we'll seek it from the other party. I've located her. The name is Kirsten Hiller."

Bob said, "I hate to do that to Sherry out of the blue. Learning of a potential sibling may be a shock. And I hope there's no need to tell her that we suspect her mom was murdered."

"I'll leave that up to you but if it should come to a murder trial, she will have to know. Speaking of which, when talking with the hit-and-run witness, I gave her a heads-up that she may get subpoenaed to a trial eventually.

I also told her that until then, she was not permitted to talk to anyone about the so-called accident she witnessed. And I warned her not to speak to any strangers, period."

He chuckled and added, "The old lady seemed to be intimidated by me. She looked like a scared little rabbit throughout the interview."

Bob took in the other's intense eyes, the scar down his face, and the sheer size of the man, and imagined how the lady must have felt. He said, "I don't understand the 'stranger bit.' Please explain it to me."

"Isn't that obvious? There's a chance that she'll get approached by the suspect, or the hired gun, in order to determine what precisely she witnessed."

"You think she's also in danger?"

"I wouldn't go that far. She can't describe the person since the vehicle had tinted windows, and with the license plates missing, the owner of the car can't be identified. I would wager an entire month's earnings that the damage to the SUV has been fixed and the vehicle is painted a different color by now."

There remained the matter of the first payment installment. Bob tried not to look pained as he glanced at the total amount of the detailed invoice Hawk handed him.

CHAPTER 42

Informing Sherry of her potential sibling situation was a delicate matter. Bob rehearsed his call to her numerous times before he dialed, only to be connected to voicemail. He left a message to the effect that he had important news for her.

Sherry retrieved it when coming home from work with a huge stack of students' papers to correct. She had been trying, and almost succeeding, to forget about the Acorn Forest Apartments and all they signified by putting all her energy into her job. So Bob's message was less than welcome. She thought, what news could he have at this point that would interest me? Might as well get it over with, she determined, and returned his call.

He picked up on the second ring and, as he thanked her for calling back, she cut him short and said, "So Mr. Tully, what's the important news?"

"I know that you're aware my friend Gloria Morris was killed by a hit-and-run driver while walking her dog."

"We've discussed that before, and I'm truly sorry for your loss."

"I suspect that she was run over on purpose to prevent her from talking with you."

"That's hard to believe."

"There's someone who wants to prevent the past from being exposed at all costs. I've hired a private investigator to get to the bottom of it all."

Sherry said, "I don't understand what you mean about the past, and what has it got to do with me?"

"I'm in the possession of Gloria's diary and some of its content concerns you."

"Really?"

Bob cleared his throat and was glad she could not see the sweat running down his face from nervous anticipation of what he was about to tell her. "It's a sensitive matter and may come as a shock to you."

"I'm a big girl."

"Okay, here it comes: you may have a half-sister."

"Oh, that! I already know it for a fact. I confess that I initially told a white lie when making you believe that I was writing my memoir. In reality, I was searching for information that would confirm my having another sibling besides my brother."

So she went ahead and told him about how she found Kirsten, and that they knew for sure they were half-sisters, as established by the DNA they sent in to Peckingline. She kept the other DNA samples and their proof as to who fathered whom to herself, as she did not think it was any of Bob Tully's business.

Bob was relieved to learn that she already knew about Kirsten and at the same time worried where their conversation may lead to next.

Sure enough, she continued, "You're the one who first told me about the husband/wife swapping that went on in those days. You may be appalled at the immorality of Kirsten's and my parents, but that doesn't justify hiring a private eye. So what else did you learn from that diary?"

There was a long pause on the line and Sherry wondered if he was still there. Finally, he said, "Gloria suspected foul play where your mom's drowning was concerned."

"No!" was the only word she got out.

"I'm so sorry to have hit you with this."

"I don't believe it. The woman must have been mistaken." And after a moment's hesitation, she said, "I want to see that diary."

"Not just yet. If there's proof of Gloria's accusations at the end of the private detective's investigation, you may see it."

When they ended the call, Sherry stared into space and thought, I wish I'd left the whole thing alone after I got back from our vacation in Hawaii.

Despite the knowledge that Hawk only liked to conduct business in person, Bob sent him the following text message: *No need to do a DNA check on Sherry and Kirsten. The two have already done so. They are half-sisters.*

CHAPTER 43

Bob made a resolution to call Kurt Morris. The man had a right to know what had resulted in connection with his mother's death. The question was how to break the news to him, and how much of it. Should he tell him about Hawk's investigation? He would make that decision on the spur of the moment as their talk progressed. He also did not want any hassle from Ralph, who was of the opinion that he was meddling in matters that were none of his concern. So he waited until Thursday evening, September 17, as soon as Ralph went to the gym, to make the call.

He started with elaborating on how happy he was to be the owner of the exquisite chess set he'd inherited from Gloria. When Kurt remarked that the sentiment had already been more than covered when he had taken possession of the set, Bob knew it was time to get to the nitty gritty.

He said, "The reason for my call is to let you know that I recovered your mother's diary from the Goodwill people."

"Good for you. I hope you enjoyed reading it," said Kurt.

"To a certain extent, but there are some troublesome disclosures in it. The diary starts with Gloria's marriage and spans over the rest of her life. The disturbing part refers to when she resided at the Acorn Forest Apartments in San Remo."

"Disturbing in what way?"

Bob gave a rough account of the text relating to the murder accusation.

"That's indeed disturbing and comes as a surprise. Mom never mentioned this to me, not at the time or later."

"You were a teenager at the time of Emma Andino's drowning, and I don't think she would have felt comfortable discussing it with you. And since she had no proof, she thought it best to keep it to herself, period."

"I guess so."

"There is more that worries me. But let me ask you first, have the police caught the person who drove the hit-and-run SUV?"

"Not yet."

Bob continued, "Your mother had an appointment to be interviewed by Sherry Rinaldi, who is Emma Andino's daughter, three days after she was killed."

"According to what you just told me you read in Mom's diary, Emma Andino was the woman who drowned in the apartments' pool. What the heck are you hinting at?"

"I believe that Gloria was run down on purpose so she couldn't expose the past to Sherry, meaning it would call into question the drowning by accident record and lead to a murder investigation."

There was a long silence, and then Kurt said, "I'm having a hard time taking all this in." And after another pause he asked, "What do you suggest we do?"

Bob had to make up his mind in a hurry with his answer. After a barely noticeable halt, he stated, "I have already hired a private investigator. If there is foul play involved, he'll find evidence. If not, we'll lay it all down to rest."

Kurt stated, "As I said, I'm having a hard time dealing with your news. May I see the diary?"

"Of course, your mother's journal belongs to you and is yours to keep. But it will have to wait. In case there's a trial, the diary needs to go into evidence."

That established, they ended the call.

CHAPTER 44

Hawk spent days doing tedious research into the suspect's past. Lots of it was irrelevant to his goal, but he had to dig hard in order to separate the worthwhile information from the useless. Although his target seemed to lead a blameless and aboveboard life, Hawk finally found a remote link the person had to the mob and pursued it. It so happened that the individual accused in the diary had a tie to a former organized crime member.

The ex-mobster's name was Victor Cirillo, who had served time in prison for racketeering; namely fencing racket, numbers racket, and drug dealing. He was never convicted of murder, but rumor had it that he did not shy away from being a gun for hire on occasion. All that was old history. After being released from prison, the man stayed away from crime, and it seemed that he had turned a new leaf. Victor now owned a legitimate business and was licensed to work in plumbing, heating, air conditioning, and electrical.

His address in a residential area in the city of Long Beach was easy to obtain. Hawk drove there in the early morning on Monday, September 21. It turned out to be a middle-class neighborhood with single family homes and a few condominiums scattered in.

Hawk's target lived in a duplex on a cul-de-sac street. He parked his car across the street along the curb and waited. At 7:45 Victor's garage door rolled open and he drove out in a pickup truck and continued down the street. Before the garage door closed again, Hawk got a glimpse of a red SUV parked inside. In case there were more people sharing the residence, the private investigator gave the surveillance some more time.

At 8:10, the front door opened and a young man emerged, walked to an older-model Toyota parked on the street, and drove off. By 8:30, Hawk figured that this was about all the traffic he'd likely witness coming out of that house. He walked over to the other duplex residence and rang the neighbor's doorbell. He was in luck. An elderly couple lived there, and when he flashed the friendly lady of the house his credentials, mentioning that he was investigating a case, she invited him in. He followed her into the kitchen, where her husband sat reading the paper, still in his robe and finishing his morning coffee.

She said, "This is Hank, a private detective, who wants to talk to us." Hawk did not correct her about his name; keeping a low profile was fine by him.

The lady shoved the breakfast dishes out of the way and motioned him into a seat. The eighty-four-year-old man looked up from his paper and asked, "What's this about?"

Hawk said, "What can you tell me about your neighbor, Victor Cirillo?"

"Not much. He owns his own business as a plumber - - or is it heating and air conditioning?"

"Both, I think," said his wife. "We don't know him well. He keeps to himself."

"How long have you folks lived here?"

"Over forty years," she replied with pride.

"And how long has Victor Cirillo been your neighbor?"

She looked up to the ceiling, figuring it out, and then said, "Must be close to five years by now. What has he done?"

"That's what I'm trying to establish. I may have the wrong lead and Mr. Cirillo may be innocent of the crime I'm investigating. Are there other people in his household?"

"Just his son, who's attending community college and seems a nice young man."

Hawk inquired, "Have you noticed any unusual activities next door?"

"No," she said, "there are no suspicious comings and goings. No questionable women, or men, for that matter. As I mentioned, they keep to themselves. Are you looking into some kind of a sex crime?"

Hawk put up both hands and reassured her, "You misunderstood. I meant nothing of that sort. I just thought that, since you folks look like a retired couple who are at home a lot, you might have noticed something out of the ordinary. As to what I'm investigating, I'm sorry, but I can't disclose that at the moment."

"I don't recall anything unusual," she answered.

The old man, who so far had not said much - - and Hawk was not sure if he even paid attention - - now jumped in by commenting, "I saw something weird the other day, and I even told my wife about it at the time. Victor was driving the gray SUV into his garage, and on the next morning, he drove out of it with the same car, only now it was red. When I told my better half here, she said I was making it up. But later on that day, when she saw Victor drive the red car back into the garage for herself, she gave me credit for being observant."

He added, "It may not be a crime, but I still think it's odd that the man gave his SUV an overnight paint job in his own garage."

Hawk said, "That *is* strange. Does he drive other vehicles?"

The octogenarian chuckled and stated, "You should know, since you sat across the street and saw him drive away in his truck!"

"Wow! You *are* observant!"

"I noticed your car parked there as Victor drove off when I first got up, and then later just happened to glance out the window again when you stepped out of your Jeep and came over to our house."

"You would make an excellent witness in a court of law," Hawk remarked.

"I hope it won't come to that," the other replied.

When Hawk got up to leave, the lady said, "Sorry we couldn't be of more help."

"Oh, you've helped, all right. And please keep this interview between us."

****

When Hawk was out the door, the lady turned to her husband and said, "He was quite nice for an alarming looking fellow. I suspect he carried a gun under his jacket."

"Since when have looks got anything to do with disposition? And you're right about the gun, but that's called for in his line of work."

"What do you think this is all about?"

"I have no idea. Maybe stolen cars, since the guy was so interested in what vehicles Victor drives."

"Do you suppose Victor is dangerous?"

"He always seemed harmless to me. And even if he's involved in some kind of a crime, I'm sure we're in no danger since we don't know anything."

And he held up his pointer finger for emphasis and said, "Make sure you tell nobody about us talking with this Hank guy."

CHAPTER 45

Hawk showed up at Bob and Ralph's home once more to report the latest findings and to receive payment for his services. He gave an account of his extensive research and then elaborated on what he had witnessed during the stakeout at Victor Cirillo's residence, and also what he had learned from the next-door neighbors.

Bob said, "Good! You found and located the hired assassin. So what is next on your agenda?"

"I think at this point, involving the authorities is called for. They need to obtain a search warrant. If there is any evidence left at Cirillo's residence to connect him to the paint job on his car, time is of the upmost importance."

Bob nodded and asked, "What indication linking Cirillo to our suspect can you give the police?"

"That's easy. As I mentioned in my report, Cirillo Junior is what ties the two together. Their shared history is well known and documented. Junior lives with his dad now, by the way. I saw him come out of the duplex."

"And we have the diary to show the police."

"It's enough to demonstrate to them where we got our information, but I don't know if it will hold up in court. The journal could be construed as circumstantial or hearsay evidence. If Gloria Morris were alive, her testimony would have a greater impact." And there was a smirk on his stark face as he added, "But we wouldn't be sitting here discussing the case if not for her fatality."

Bob could not bring himself to laugh at the joke.

Hawk continued, "The police no doubt will order their own DNA testing, including matching up each parent's DNA against the daughters'. We know, or at least can take an educated guess, of the outcome, but they need solid proof."

"So you're positive that we can give the police enough information for them to start an official investigation?"

"To do so and follow our lead is in their best interest. As of today, they haven't made any progress in catching the hit-and-run driver. So they'll be more than happy for the tip. And since the silencing of your friend is a direct consequence of the drowning that happened 40 years ago, they cannot ignore the first murder either."

Bob said, "That makes sense." And he asked, "Do we let Sherry and her half-sister know about getting the authorities involved?"

"Are you out of your mind?" Hawk roared. "We don't want the suspect or the hired gun to be warned off and take a chance of either one skipping town. You need to keep a lid on this." And he tagged him with an accusing stare, asking, "Who else besides Sherry Rinaldi knows about what you hired me for?"

Scared now, Bob replied, "Just Ralph, my partner, and I also told Kurt Morris, Gloria's son."

"Tell them to keep their mouths shut."

CHAPTER 46

Hawk got the authorities aboard the very next day. His evidence and Cirillo's phone records were enough cause to obtain a search warrant for Victor Cirillo's home. Two police officers showed up and blocked him in on the driveway, as he was about to leave in his truck on the way to a plumbing job. The house search showed nothing of interest, but they found spray paint equipment and leftover red paint in the garage, as well as the tools that had been used on the bumper damage. The garage also still smelled of spray-paint, even though its window was kept wide open.

Cirillo's red SUV was parked inside the two-car garage and the authorities informed him that they were calling for a tow-truck to confiscate it for evidence.

"Wait a minute," Cirillo shouted, "I know my rights! You can't just haul away my SUV. There's nothing illegal about spray-painting one's own car."

"Correct. But killing a victim by hit-and-run is illegal. And trying to cover it up by fixing the damage to the car and repainting it a different color makes the first crime at least manslaughter."

"Who claims I did a hit-and-run?"

"We have evidence to that effect," one of the officer's replied.

Victor was not ready to give up yet and demanded, "I'd like to hear about it."

"You will in due course."

The tow-truck drove up at that moment, drowning out Cirillo's next remark. With the SUV towed away minutes later, the two officers left also with the warning, "You are put under surveillance. Any attempt to leave town will result in your immediate arrest. Is that clear?"

"Sure, I get it," Victor replied. And he thought, I know the routine - - been there, done it!

****

Upon examination in their lab, technicians discovered dark gray paint beneath the layer of red paint on Victor Cirillo's SUV. That - - together with evidence given them by Hawk, phone records, and interviewing his neighbors and the hit-and-run witness - - was sufficient for Cirillo's apprehension. On Friday morning, September 25, the same two police officers interrupted the breakfast he shared with his son. They read him his Miranda Rights and placed him under arrest for the murder of Gloria Morris.

CHAPTER 47

On the following Monday evening, Dave was on his commute home from work. Life was good and back to normal again, he mused. The pressing job-related deadline was met and for the moment he and his co-workers could relax. At home, all was well also. Sherry and he had enjoyed the weekend with a rewarding hike in the local San Gabriel Mountains on Saturday, and attended a matinee musical on Sunday.

His Sherry was back to being her normal, pleasant self, no longer brooding over the past. She had even picked up sewing once again, whenever her teaching job yielded free time. Consequently, he was not prepared for what awaited him when arriving home.

Dave found Sherry in total panic, showering him with sentences that came out of her mouth like explosions.

She rattled on, "When I got home from school, the police were waiting for me at the front door. I let them in and they informed me that Mom's drowning was under investigation. Can you believe it? They bombarded me with all sorts of questions and even seemed to know about the DNA testing Kirsten and I have done. I asked who set off their investigation but they said that was confidential."

"Slow down! What exactly about the drowning is under investigation?"

"They said it may not have been an accident."

"Do they mean she committed suicide?"

"Get real! There would have been far easier ways to kill herself than slamming her head into the pool wall on purpose. Of course they mean that somebody else killed her!"

And before Dave got a chance to process the news, Sherry went on, "Back in July, I had this horrible dream about a woman being hit with a baseball bat and then pushed into a pool where she drowned. I tried to forget about the nightmare but today, while the police were here, the ghastly image crept back into my mind."

"So sorry, Honey, that you have to deal with this. But the dream was just a dream, nothing more."

As if she had not heard his comment, Sherry continued, "After the officers left, I thought about it long and hard. The only person who knew about my quest and the DNA samples, besides Kirsten, was Bob Tully. The other day he called, letting me know he had hired a private investigator. I was in denial at the time but now it is real. The PI must be the one who got the police involved."

"What made Bob do that? I mean, what was there to investigate, since he already knew that you and Kirsten are sisters. And most of all, what has it got to do with Bob?"

"Gloria Morris was a good friend of his."

"And who is Gloria Morris?"

"She was the woman I wanted to interview but got killed by a hit-and-run driver before I could do so. Bob told me that he had Gloria's diary, where she suggested that Mom was murdered. I didn't believe it for a moment and dismissed it, and the fact that he hired a private eye, from my mind."

Lifting her troubled eyes up to him, she cried out, "Now that the police are conducting a formal investigation, I can't ignore it any longer. Oh, how I wish that I'd listened to you from day one and left it all alone!"

****

Ben called his sister that same evening and instead of asking, "Hello, how are you?" he yelled, "What the hell is going on? The police showed up at our house informing me that Mom's drowning was under investigation. If this has anything to do with your so-called project, you have gone insane! No matter what kind of idiotic woman's intuition made you call the authorities, you had no right to do so."

Sherry was about to set him straight but could not get a word out before he raged on, "When I asked what prompted the investigation four decades later, one of the officers said it was linked to a current case. It goes without saying that they were not authorized to tell me about that current case. And obviously I could not give them any useful information, as I was five years old at the time.

"I'm asking you again, what the hell is this all about? I always thought we were a normal family. Murder does not happen in normal families."

Sherry said, "I can understand that you're angry and that this caught you out of the blue. I was upset too when the officers came to my house and still am now."

"You could hardly have been surprised, since you instigated it," he shot back.

"I've been trying to tell you; I did not call the authorities."

"Then who did?"

Sherry was left with no choice but to come clean with it all and told the complex story: how she arrived at finding her half-sister, getting Bob Tully involved, the hit-and-run alleged fatal accident of Gloria Morris, and Bob's hiring of a private investigator.

After she had spelled it all out he said, "This sounds like a complicated plot in a movie. I can't believe it's real and involves our family."

"It's all my fault. I wish that I'd left it alone from the beginning."

"Does Dad know?"

Sherry replied, "He knows that I know about the husband/wife swapping and that there is a chance that I'm not his flesh and blood. As for the rest, I don't think he knows about the killing of Gloria Morris or that there is a police investigation, unless they have interviewed him too. Come to think of it, they most likely have, or will."

There was silence on the line for a moment and then Ben stated, "So it turns out that he's not your dad and you're only my half-sister. I'm having a hard time accepting that. And what is even more appalling is the idea that Mom was murdered."

"How do you think this is all affecting me?" Sherry said, bursting into tears and ending the call.

CHAPTER 48

At first, the interrogation of Victor Cirillo did not go well. He refused to talk without his attorney present. His lawyer came and talked to him in private, giving marginal advice, which came down to, "Don't admit to anything," and then left. So the authorities let their suspect stew in his cell for a couple days, giving him time to think what would be in his best interest, before questioning him again.

The detective assigned to the case was Lieutenant Andrew Sharplander, known as Sharpy to his inner circle. The nickname came from his name and the sharp mind he was known for. Of average height and middle aged, the lieutenant's laid-back disposition and seemingly friendly interrogation methods generated good results, more often than not.

He walked into the interrogation room with an outstretched hand, announcing, "Hello, Mr. Cirillo. I'm Andrew Sharplander, and I'm going to ask you some questions related to the murder of Gloria Morris. I must caution you that our conversation is being recorded."

Victor did not get out of his chair but reluctantly shook the offered hand, and without prompting said, "I did not even know this Gloria Morris I'm being accused of killing."

"Oh, I believe you, but the person who hired you to do so surely knew her," Sharplander stated, sitting down and facing him across the table that stood between them.

"You may have me for the hit-and-run, but you can't prove that I did it on purpose or was a hired gun. I know the law; you can't hold my past record against me which, as you well know, was not for murder. I've served my time and led a blameless life ever since my release from prison years ago."

"So true," the lieutenant agreed, "until Monday, August 17, at 9:13 a.m., when you ran over Gloria Morris at full speed, while she and her dog were in the crosswalk in plain view."

"You have no proof," Victor said, staring him down.

"We have a witness."

"Oh, the old woman; I bet she's half blind."

As soon as the remark was out, Victor realized what a huge blunder he'd made, and paled. His interrogator's face, by comparison, turned into a big grin.

Victor tried to soften the blow by adding, "I meant, no one can prove I did it on purpose."

Looking at some spot on the wall, the lieutenant stated, "Let the record show that Mr. Cirillo is aware of having been seen by a witness when running Gloria Morris over with his SUV."

Focusing his eyes back on Victor, he said, "You have no verifiable alibi on the date in question from around 8:10

a.m., as you and your son left your residence - - you in the SUV and he in the Toyota - - and when your neighbor saw you coming back at 10:05 a.m. More than enough time to drive from your home in Long Beach to the scene of the crime and back."

Victor pinned the detective with a defying stare and said, "What about motive? You can't come up with one."

"The person who hired you had a strong motive for silencing Gloria Morris. We have established a connection between you and that partner in crime of yours."

"What connection?"

"It goes back to the years you served in prison. Since your wife had died from an overdose, you were the sole provider for your three-year-old son, who would have gone through the social services process, had it not been for the generosity of that person who gave him a home and did an excellent job of bringing him up."

"Okay, that was easy for you to dig up, but it doesn't make me a hired assassin by a long shot."

Sharplander looked at the spot on the wall again and stated, "We have recent phone records between the two of you." And with a sudden jerk out of his chair, he leaned across the table and placed his face three inches from Victor and whispered, "I suppose you don't even know why you were hired."

Victor shook his head.

"I thought so! I'm going to enlighten you." And the lieutenant addressed the wall and said, "I need the excerpt."

Moments later, a uniformed officer came into the room, handed his superior some paperwork, and stepped out again without uttering a word. Left to themselves, the detective pointed to the three pages in front of him and said, "What I have here is a transcript from an excerpt of Gloria Morris' diary." And he read it aloud:

"*Friday, May 30, 1980*

I overheard a bit of interesting news today. After coming home from work, I was doing a couple loads of laundry. The laundry room door was wide open and I looked out the window while folding the clothes I had taken out of the dryer. I saw Emma and Louise's husband - - I forgot his name - - watching their little girls in the playground. The kids were swinging side by side, with the older one able to pump by herself, while Emma gave her toddler an occasional push.

And here is what I overheard: Emma said, 'You must be aware that our girls look alike.' He laughed and agreed, 'Now that you mention it, I see the resemblance. What a coincidence.'

'It may not be.'

'What do you suggest?'

'Surely you remember what happened more than two and a half years ago.'

He lowered his voice a tad but the window and door to the laundry room was open, and I could hear him saying, 'Oh, the little mishap. You don't think - - -'

'Yes, I do. There is a chance that Sherry is yours. I've been thinking about it a lot, especially lately, when I see the two play together. We need to tell our spouses.'

He said, 'Don't jump to conclusions.'

'My mind is made up, I'm going to tell my husband and you need to tell Louise. If you don't, I will!'

He shot back, 'Don't say anything yet. We need to discuss this further. I'll meet you by the pool tonight.'

At that point, I was done with the laundry and walked out the door, carrying the basket. The man made eye contact with me as I passed the playground, and I could tell that he knew that I had overheard their conversation.

I thought to myself, interesting indeed! I can put two and two together. Sherry is around two years old, and nine months before then the wife/husband swapping around here was in full swing."

He paused, and continued:

"Saturday, May 31, 1980

There was a horrible accident last night. Emma Andino drowned in the apartment complex's pool. I feel tremendous compassion for her husband, poor man. And the kids, Ben and Sherry, will have to grow up without a mother."

He paused again, then continued:

"Saturday, June 14, 1980

I've been thinking, what if Emma's drowning was not an accident at all? I keep remembering the words I overheard Olov Ericson speak - - I do remember his first name now - - 'I'll meet you by the pool tonight.' The fact that she drowned that same night can't be a coincidence. Shall I come forward and tell the authorities what I overheard? Mulling it over, I understand that I have no evidence and that I could do more harm than good by making an accusation.

This morning, I ran into him. Our parking spots are next to each other. The look he gave me was confirmation that he was aware that I knew.

Before I could control myself, the words were out and I said, 'For the two girls' sake and both families involved, I will keep silent.' He said, 'What are you talking about?' To which I replied,

'Don't act innocent.' 'What do you want?' he hissed. And to my utter disgust I realized that he thought I was blackmailing him.

I replied, 'Absolutely nothing. Like I said, I'm thinking of the little girls.'

'Me too,' he stated, unlocked his car and drove off. With a heavy heart I locked mine and walked in the direction of my apartment.

And now, sitting here, writing it all down, I wonder if I have made the right decision. I mean, the man is getting away with murder."

Victor had paid keen attention to what was read to him and thought, shit, the judge killed a woman. No wonder he wanted me to silence Gloria Morris, who knew about it. But why wait 40 years? The question was so mindboggling to him that he could not stop himself. He asked, "Waiting four decades to do something about it is hard to believe."

Sharplander replied, "You're getting to the gist of the matter. It turns out that the two girls concerned - - women by now - - figured out that they were half-sisters and Olov Ericson realized that the whole past would come to light. But let's get to what concerns *you*. As you can see, the cat is out of the bag and if you cooperate, you may get off with a lighter sentence."

Victor stayed silent and mulled it over. Did he owe the judge any loyalty? No longer, he decided. And anyhow, it was Louise Ericson who had brought about opening her home to Vinny and who had taken him under her wing for many years, not the judge. It was thanks to the judge's wife that Vinny had enjoyed a carefree life during those crucial years instead of being passed around to foster homes.

He knew that the game was up and hated the thought of going back to prison. Once he was released after serving his sentence, he had cut all ties to the mob. And most important, had gotten used to being an upright, respected citizen who enjoyed working and owning his one-man business. What crazy idea had made him think he owed it to the judge to take on the hit job in the first place? If he could cut some years off his sentence now, he'd take the deal.

The interrogation went on for another half hour, but it was only a formality. They both knew the outcome. In the end, Victor Cirillo confessed to the murder of Gloria Morris under contract from Olov Ericson. With his lawyer present, he cut a deal for less prison time, due to his full cooperation.

CHAPTER 49

On Tuesday, September 29, Lieutenant Sharplander together with a uniformed officer arrested Judge Olov Ericson at his home. It was an unconventional arrest, but the circumstances and the person who was being taken into custody led to the unusual procedure. On the drive to Irvine, Detective Sharplander considered that he did not like the errand one bit. He had come in contact with Judge Ericson on several occasions in the past and knew him as a fair and compassionate upholder of the law. What had transpired with this current case had shocked the lieutenant to the core, and he had a hard time accepting it, even when faced with the facts.

Showing up with a warrant for the judge's arrest at the courthouse would have been cruel, the detective thought, so he waited until the early evening when he could count on finding him at home. As the door was opened to them, they were greeted by furious barking from Ember, who clearly mistrusted the uniformed officer.

Judge Ericson calmed the Schnauzer down, invited them in, and then said, "Hello, Sharpy! What brings you by?"

"Judge Olov Ericson, I'm sorry to inform you that I have a warrant for your arrest for the murder of Emma Andino, and the hiring of an assassin for the murder of Gloria Morris."

The judge's pleasant smile vanished and his expression turned to dread as he said, "So you caught Victor and he confessed. I don't blame him; he has to look out for himself." And with a sad nod he added, "I'm coming willingly, but give me some time. I need to talk with my wife, who deserves an explanation."

The lieutenant looked at his watch and said, "I'll give you 15 minutes, your Honor."

"Thanks, Sharpy!"

He found Louise in the kitchen, preparing dinner. She asked, "Who was ringing the doorbell?"

"Please turn off the gas range and sit down," he replied.

She turned to look at his grave face, did as advised, and then asked, "It's all coming out, isn't it?"

He sat down at the kitchen table to face her and replied, "Yes, the authorities are here to arrest me for the murder of Emma. You never said anything but I think you suspected."

She nodded.

"It was a freak accident. The condom broke and I never gave it a thought until one day when Emma and I were watching the girls on the playground. She mentioned the resemblance and suggested that I might be the father of her Sherry. I didn't want to believe it, but she insisted that we tell our spouses. She even threatened that if I wouldn't, she'd do so herself.

"Under no circumstances did I want you to know about the possibility that Sherry was my kid. Not only had you been against joining the swapping couples and resented that I had managed to talk you into connecting with the group, but you had also been longing for another child, which the doctors told you was no longer possible after Kirsten. I was positive that you'd have divorced me if you knew."

He gave her a pleading look and continued, "I loved you and didn't want to lose you. And I admit that I could also not afford to. You supported me financially while I attended law school, and your parents were going to help us buy our first house."

Louise was about to say something, but he held up his hand and continued, "Let me finish my confession. We don't have much time. On the day Emma informed me of her suspicion, I told her to meet me at the pool at night to discuss the matter further before telling our spouses. I swear that I planned to only talk it over with her and try to change her mind, nothing more. The pool area was deserted at that late hour and I first waited for her by the deck table and chairs. When she didn't show up right away for her usual evening lap swimming, I went for a dip in the pool myself.

"I heard her come in the gate, walk over, dive in, and start her laps. I waited at the deep-end for her, but she ignored me, made her turn, and kept going. That pissed me off, but I decided to let her do her thing until she was ready to talk with me. I watched her do several laps. She seemed to be in a swimming frenzy, and I realized that she was angry and first needed to let off steam. When at long last she came to a halt next to me, I said, 'Let's talk it over, please.' She replied, 'If you mean telling our spouses that you are most likely Sherry's father, there is nothing to talk about. They need to know.'"

He shot a desperate look Louise's way and went on, "I tried to reason with her, mentioning that what they didn't know couldn't hurt them. Emma insisted that you and her husband had a right to know, and what would happen next was up to you and him. It was too dark in the pool to make out the expression on her face, but I could tell by her tone of voice that she was angry. I said that my telling you that I might have fathered someone else's child was out of the question, and she had the nerve to threaten me again by saying that if I would not confess to you, she certainly would. And then she hinted that she herself may already have told Max."

He sighed and continued, "What followed, I remember word for word and action by action, like it was yesterday. 'You're bluffing,' I said. She shot back, 'Maybe, and maybe not,' and took off swimming again. At that point an ear-throbbing rage came over me. As she swam back toward me at the deep end of the pool, about to make her turn back, I grabbed her by the shoulder and rammed her head into the pool edge as hard as I could. When I realized that I'd knocked her unconscious and she was going under, I just watched instead of coming to her rescue."

Sighing again, the judge came to the end of his sordid story and said, "I didn't mean to kill her, the entire thing happened like in a dream. I believe that I could have saved her but lost my head and watched her drown."

After a pause he looked Louise in the eye and said, "You knew, correct?"

"I suspected," she replied. "There was this photo taken at the Acorn Forest Apartments, showing several couples with their children, the Andinos and us included. Other than being a year apart in age, Kirsten and Sherry looked alike. In fact, they looked like you. As for the rest, I had gone to bed early that night but heard you come home and then open the patio sliding-glass door. Remember, it squeaked? I was curious, waited until you were asleep, and then went to investigate. I found your dripping swimming trunks flung over a patio chair. I thought, so that's all, he went for a swim, and forgot about it. Later, when the news of Emma's drowning accident was the talk of the apartment complex, I remembered that you had gone to the pool on that night."

"Why didn't you say something?" the judge asked.

"I wasn't sure. And as weeks, months, and years went by, I tried to put it out of my mind."

He touched her hand lightly and stated, "But you could not. Ergo your depression. I was never able to figure out what went on inside your head, since you were aloof most of the time. It wasn't until the other day, when you asked whether there was no statute of limitations on murder, that I got an inkling."

She did not respond and he continued, "I should have at least tried to save her, but I panicked and got out of the water and ran home. No matter what, I should have called the authorities, but I was too much of a coward. Even a verdict of manslaughter would have landed me in prison. I told myself that I kept quiet because of you and Kirsten, but I was kidding myself. In reality, I was worried about only me and my future. My legal career would have gone down the drain.

"When a few days went by and Max Andino did not confront me, I was sure that Emma had not told him about our mishap of over two and a half years earlier. There was only one person who knew. That was Gloria Morris."

"I remember her," Louise interrupted. "She was the local gossip."

"Right. I won't go into details, but Gloria knew and I first thought she wanted to blackmail me. She didn't, however, and told me that she'd keep my secret for the two families' sake."

He looked at his watch and rapidly went on, "I have only a few minutes left, so I'd better get to the more recent events. My crime was dormant for so many years that I was almost able to forget it ever happened. When Sherry contacted Kirsten, I knew that together they would uncover and expose the past. The only person who could point the finger at me was Gloria Morris, and I hoped that she had passed away. I did some research and discovered that she was still alive. Again, I panicked and engaged Victor to silence her, which was a gross mistake. As you can see, I'm paying the price. They have already arrested Victor."

He heard Louise gasp but ignored it and went on, "I'm ashamed of it all and sorry that I've hurt you in the process."

There was no longer anything vague about Louise, who had paid keen attention during her husband's admissions. She now glared at him and stated, "That was excellent acting on your part on the day you told me about the letter Kirsten had received from Sherry. When Emma Andino's name came up, you pretended to have forgotten who she was."

Then she pointed an accusing finger at him and said, "How could you order Victor to do such a horrible thing!

He was a law-abiding citizen in all the years after his release from prison. I can't even imagine what his arrest and what follows will do to Vinny. And I'm frightened of what yours will do to Kirsten."

Focused and in total command she added, "Your problem was that you were driven by ambition. Your career meant more to you than people's lives."

Her spouse was about to make a reply when Lieutenant Sharplander showed up at the door, saying, "Time is up, Judge Ericson."

The judge got out of his chair, went to bend over his wife, and while hugging her whispered in her ear, "Please forgive me, Louise. And tell Kirsten not to hate me." Then he turned to the detective with arms outstretched and said, "Let's go, Sharpy."

The detective noticed the gesture and stated, "We can skip the handcuffs, sir."

As Lieutenant Sharplander and the uniformed officer escorted Olov Ericson out of his home and to the waiting unmarked police car, he thought, no doubt the judge will be convicted. He is 67 now, so it is certain that he'll die in prison. Victor Cirillo, now in his mid-forties, will be an old man when he gets out, if he ever does.

CHAPTER 50

Despite Sharplander's efforts to keep the judge's arrest out of the public eye, the news leaked to the media and Louise did not dare step out their front door where newscasters and paparazzi gathered.

On the following Saturday a phone conversation took place between Louise and her daughter. After the first emotional exchange, their talk ended by Kirsten asking, "Where is Dad now?"

Louise replied, "Out on bail." And she moaned, "We have to sneak out the back door and cross over to the neighbor's property when taking Ember for a walk. Can you come by? I could use your support and you and I could help one another cope."

The anger in Kirsten's voice was evident when she shot back, "I can't face Dad right now and be civil, maybe I never will. Why don't you come and stay with us for a few days? It may do you good."

Louise took her up on it and drove to San Diego on Monday, October 5.

****

The kids were in school and Mike was on active duty getting a local brush fire under control. Kirsten called in sick and arranged for another real estate agent to take her place for the day. She now faced her mom at the opposite side of her kitchen's center aisle, each sitting on a cushioned stool. Intent on their talk, they forgot to drink the tea that Kirsten had brewed and let it get cold.

Kirsten had planned to console Louise when extending her invitation, but now it looked like her mom was doing most of the consoling. In fact, for the first time in years there was nothing vague about Louise. She was focused and in control.

Kirsten pinned her with an accusing stare and said, "You knew all along, didn't you? That's why you withdrew to a world of your own."

"I suspected but wasn't sure."

"We haven't told the kids yet." And she burst out, "How do we tell them that their grandpa is a murderer?"

"I'll do it gently, if you wish."

Without acknowledging the offer, Kirsten continued, "He's a judge, for crying out loud! How could he sit in judgement of people when he himself committed the crime of all crimes?"

"Maybe the reason he was such an excellent judge is because he had compassion for both the victim and the accused. I'm not trying to diminish his action but he did not premeditate Emma Andino's murder. It happened out of spur-of-the-moment rage." And she shared the confession her husband had made to her on the day of his arrest.

Kirsten did not interrupt and waited until her mom's exposé came to an end and then asked, "Would you have divorced him, had you known that he fathered Sherry?"

"The answer is no. I suspected that long before Emma's drowning, since I noticed that her daughter looked like you. I was waiting for your dad to mention the possibility, but he never did. He obviously had put the accident he and Emma had had out of his mind and only remembered it after his confrontation with her, some two and a half years later."

Kirsten said, "I have a confession of my own to make. Sherry and I already knew that Max Andino is not her father but Dad is." And she told about the DNA samples she had obtained behind their backs and sent to Peckingline for cross matching.

Louise sighed and remarked, "So at least that part of the revelation did not come as a shock to you."

"No, but the murders sure did," Kirsten shot back.

Her mom glanced around the state-of-the-art kitchen and took a sip of her tea, ignoring that it was cold.

She stated, "I could maybe forgive his first crime, but what he ordered Victor Cirillo to do is unforgivable. What this must do to Vinny breaks my heart."

"Have you talked with him since his dad's arrest?"

"I've tried but he doesn't answer the phone. He must recognize the number and think it's the Judge calling. Or, he may not want to have anything to do with either one of us. Who could blame him? I'll have to go to their house and talk with him in person."

Kirsten stared at her mom in astonishment and said, "You're no longer passive. Instead, you're taking an interest and are in command!"

Then she got out of her stool and said, "I'll make us some fresh tea."

CHAPTER 51

Meanwhile, Sherry and Max Andino both knew that there was unfinished business which needed to be sorted out between them. Sherry wanted to let some time go by before facing him, but Max had a different idea.

He showed up unexpectedly at the Rinaldi residence on Saturday morning, following Judge Ericson's arrest.

Dave answered the door, took one look at the man he still considered his father-in-law, and said, "I can see that you need to talk with Sherry. She's in the den."

Max found her clad in workout leggings and sports bra, peddling on her stationary bicycle, working up a sweat. She waved a hand at him in greeting but did not stop.

He said, "Hi Po - - I mean Sherry - - finish your routine. I don't mind waiting."

She glanced at the bike's timer and said between labored gasps, "Just three more minutes."

He made himself comfortable on the sofa at the other end of the room and watched the young woman he now was forced to admit was not his child. The ups and downs of 42 years of fathering flashed past his mind. Overall, he had done a good job bringing her and his son up. Most of the memories he recalled were good ones, with Poker being his pride and joy. Was she going to deny the bond that existed between them and reject him now?

He was pulled out of his reverie when Sherry stepped off the bike, wiped her forehead with a towel, and plopped herself down on the sofa next to him, saying, "So you've come to clear the air between us?"

"Exactly."

"Did you know all along that Olov Ericson was my father and not you?"

"Honest to God, I did not."

Sherry glared at him and insisted, "But you lied to me when you said you didn't remember what your fight with Mom was about before she bolted to the pool the night she drowned."

Max averted his eyes, addressing the ceiling, "Yes, I lied. I remembered it clearly."

And he met her eyes again as he continued, "Here is the argument we had, and as a consequence, the last memory I have of your mother: She mentioned that there was a possibility that you were not my child and then said, 'Let me tell you how it happened,' and was about to elaborate on who she thought might have fathered you. I wanted no part of it and refused to be reasonable, yelling at her, 'I don't need to listen to any of this! Sherry is *my* child and that's all there is to it. Stop making outrageous claims!'

Her last words shouted at me before she stormed off and slammed the door behind her, were, 'Take a good look at Sherry and face reality, instead of burying your stubborn head in the sand like an ostrich! I don't like it either but am dealing with the facts.'"

There was sorrow in his eyes as he added, "I've felt guilty all along for not going after her and calming her down when I thought that she rammed her head into the pool edge full of rage by accident. Now that I know that Ericson killed her, I feel double the guilt. My being there would have prevented it."

Dave stuck his head in the door and announced, "I'm off to run some errands, see you later," and shut the door again. With minds focused on their talk, neither of the two sitting on the sofa paid attention to his announcement.

In spite of feeling compassion for the man, Sherry had to ask, "You never suspected that I was not your daughter?"

"No. We had such a strong bond between us that I couldn't accept any other possibility and believed that you were mine. Only recently, after you came back from Hawaii and then talked about a Doppelgänger who also lived in the Acorn Forest Apartments in San Remo, did I start to take your mother's claim seriously and had doubts."

"You hadn't noticed that I didn't look like anyone else in the family and was the only blonde?"

"Grandmother on your mother's side was fair."

"On the numerous occasions that I wanted to know details about Mom when growing up, I took your evasive answers as grief. Lately, I suspected it was out of guilt."

"Both are true," he said, "I mourned her loss for many years, and I felt extremely guilty for joining the swapping group. Had we not belonged to it, she would never have drowned."

Sherry realized that this was all the revelation she was going to get from him and that it was her turn to make a declaration. She said, "I have a confession to make," and told him about the DNA testing.

He smiled and stated, "I knew you'd pursue it all the way."

All of a sudden Sherry's eyes turned moist and she cried out, "I need to get something more off my chest. I had a terrifying suspicion. When I first became aware that Mom's drowning was not an accident, I thought it was you who killed her. How could I even think for a minute that you were capable of such a thing? Please forgive me."

He draped an arm around her shoulder and said, "You had just learned that I was not your father and that your mother did not drown by accident. Who could blame you for jumping to that conclusion?"

Now sobbing without restraint, she said between taking in gulps of air, "And it turns out that my actual father is the murderer!"

Max did not comment for some time, letting her have a good cry. When she was done, he reached into his trousers pocket and handed her his handkerchief.

She dried her eyes with it and in spite of all was amused. "So you still carry a cloth hankie, how wonderfully old-fashioned!"

Picking up the subject once more, he said, "Ericson may have accidentally given his semen, but I don't consider him your father. He is a stranger to you. I'm the one who raised you, loved you, nursed you when you were sick, laughed with you through good times, and stood by you during challenges for 42 years. Consequently, *I am your dad.*"

She turned to hug him as he added, "And I insist you keep calling me 'Dad.'"

"Sure, Dad, and go ahead and call me Poker. After all, I've done a lot of poking."

EPILOGUE

In June of the following year, Sherry and Kirsten got together for the first time since the distressing consequence of their discovery. Kirsten had spent two days in Orange County to help her mother move into a condominium and, before returning to San Diego, arranged to meet for lunch with her half-sister. She chose a restaurant in Irvine and asked to be seated in a booth, giving them privacy.

When settled, she said, "Today is June 18! Do you realize that exactly a year ago we met in the hotel's bathroom on Maui?"

"Our world sure changed in just one year," Sherry said. "At the time I thought it was a nice stroke of fate but now I'm not so sure."

After giving the waiter their orders of chicken Caesar salads, she asked, "How is your mom coping?"

"Quite well, to everyone's surprise," Kirsten replied. "Of course you don't know this, but she had depression issues for many years. More often than not, she retreated into a world of her own where nobody could reach her.

After Dad's arrest, she snapped right out of it, as if she were relieved to have it all come out in the open. Like a huge burden was taken off her shoulders. I saw a difference in her right away; she was in command for the first time in years."

"Amazing!"

"Not only that, but she was the one who broke the news to our kids in the most gentle way. A thing I could not bring myself to do."

She continued, "And now, after his conviction and their separation being final, she seems to face reality well. There was no reason for her to stay in their big house all alone, and I think she'll love living in her condo. I hope she makes new acquaintances, as she feels awkward around their mutual old friends."

"How are things with *you*?"

"Frankly, I've had a hard time since last September, but I'm getting better." And she pinned Sherry with a meaningful stare and admitted, "At first I was pissed at you for starting the whole thing."

"I don't blame you."

The waiter brought their salads and for a while they ate in silence. Then Kirsten took up where she had left off and said, "Then I realized that it must be just as bad for you, if not worse. First you found out that the man you thought was your dad was not. Then you had to deal with the bombshell that your real father is a killer."

Sherry did not tell her that she did not consider Olov Ericson her father and nodded in agreement.

"Besides, we'd have all been living a lie."

After they were done with lunch and sipping coffee, Kirsten said, "For months I could not bring myself to face Dad but finally went to visit him in prison, only the other day. He's remorseful and willingly accepts his punishment, knowing that he'll never be a free man again. That's why he didn't fight the charge and pleaded guilty."

She added, "He told me to ask you for forgiveness too."

Sherry nodded again and said, "Strictly speaking, I owe him my very existence."

The waiter came with the bill, and as Sherry reached for her wallet, Kirsten stopped her, saying, "Let me!"

Sherry watched Kirsten sign the credit card slip and noticed that her sister was left-handed, just as she herself was.

There was no need for more words. They had found the truth, but sometimes the truth hurts.

Stand-Alone Mysteries by Alice Zogg

Exposing the Past
No Curtain Call
The Ill-Fated Scientist
Accidental Eyewitness
A Bet Turned Deadly

R. A. Huber Mysteries by Alice Zogg

Evil at Shore Haven
Guilty or Not
Murder at the Cubbyhole
Revamp Camp
Final Stop Albuquerque
The Fall of Optimum House
The Lonesome Autocrat
Tracking Backward
Turn the Joker Around
Reaching Checkmate